BROKEN FAUN

ALEXANDRA K MARTIN

Copyright © Alexandra K. Martin 2022

First Edition 2022,

Ebook ISBN: 978-0-6450508-3-7

Paperback ISBN: 978-0-6453856-7-0

Hardback ISBN: 978-0-6453856-0-1

This novel is entirely a work of fiction. The names, characters and incidents portrayed in it are the work of the author's imagination. Any resemblance to actual persons, living or dead, events or localities is entirely coincidental.

Cover and Title Art: © DAZED Designs 2022

Editor: Melissa Plant

Formatter: © DAZED Designs 2022

"I see beauty in the bent, the rotting, the decayed, and the shattered. I find splendor in things most would find *terrifying*. I think that things that are damaged are just *exquisite*. Because I know they are just like me. They are not ruined forever; things that are broken have a funny way of being fixed and turning out better than before."

— *JORDAN SARAH WEATHERHEAD*

FOREWARNING

This is a Reverse Harem Sci-Fi/PNR novel with adult content, and is recommended for the mature audience. Reverse Harem means that the main female character can and will choose more than one partner. It may also contain some darker elements, such as violence. All in all though, this is one of my lighter, easier reads. Enjoy.

To my priceless alpha/beta team, you are the wind beneath my wings. Seriously though, without you I wouldn't be able to grow and learn, and my stories wouldn't be half of what they are now. Your constant support and understanding makes so much difference for me, and I want you to know that I'm so grateful for you.

Sandy, Amanda, Laura, Jen, Kelly, Natasha, Tanisha, Marissa and Ashley; thank you!

MAIN BROKEN GLOSSARY

*Faun-Deer

*Alfa-Wolf
*Ironside-Rhino
*Mayne-Lion
*Nanuk-Polar bear
*Sabre-Tiger
*Steve-Crocodile
*Styng-Scorpion
*Tallon-Owl
*Venom-Spider

*Sylva-Gorilla
*Adda-Snake
*Fang-Snake
*King-Lion

*Kit-Beaver
*Baabaa-Sheep

PROLOGUE
DR. FOSTER ADINA

LIKE A MOTH TO A FLAME, THE SMALL CRIES CALL TO ME FROM the nursery; and before I realize where I'm going, I'm standing in the doorway, staring down at the lines of glass cribs filling the room.

The majority of babies are quiet and content, but the trembling wail of one of the newborns pulls at my heartstrings, and I can't help but approach the tiny creature. With little fists raised in protest, the small girl, with cute horn nubs protruding from her soft golden hair, screams with all her might. Faun, as Dr. Micheals called her, is smaller than the other babies, but she's also one of the few prey spliced for the Ark program.

Faun's little face starts to turn pink with her obvious distress, and she reminds me of my own daughter as a baby. Remembering what used to settle Morigan down, I reach and softly circle her round belly, humming quietly to her. Faun's cries lessen and lessen until nothing more than short, silent quivers remain; her face now lax and her perfect pink bottom lip sucking in with her sad, shaky breathing.

"There, there, darling," I tell her gently. "You're safe, little one. I'm not going to hurt you."

I stroke her soft hand, and she grasps tightly onto my finger, her gray gaze capturing my heart. I suck in a breath and instantly know that I'm telling her the truth. What started as a fascinating government project just turned into a room of innocent children, and the reality of that smacks me hard in the chest. How did I never fully understand the repercussions of what I was doing in helping to create lives? Lives that otherwise wouldn't exist. Lives that now rely on me doing the right thing, because when I look at Faun, I don't see research; I see a little girl, much like my own, needing to be protected from a world that will never accept her as she is, and even worse, needing protection from the very place that created her.

Leaning in close, I make her a promise that one way or another I intend to keep. "One day when you need me, I'll be there for you, and I'll do everything I can to give you the freedom you deserve."

I kiss dimpled knuckles and watch in awe as she falls asleep, somehow understanding that she can trust me. Her instincts are working perfectly, even now.

CHAPTER 1
FAUN

A SMOOTH, RELAXED BREATH RELEASES FROM DEEP WITHIN MY lungs as I push back into downward dog; the action flawless after years of practice. With my eyes closed, I inhale, feeling my chest expand with the movement, when my nose suddenly twitches with a scent that is starting to become familiar to me at the oddest times, and it's both confusing and strangely arousing.

My eyes snap open, and I peer between my legs, catching my pack with all their gazes focused solely on my ass, and as suspected, the scent that makes my skin heat is coming from them. With flushing cheeks, I try to keep my focus on my breathing and not their increasingly strange behavior.

Alfa's golden wolf eyes darken, and his head tilts to the side like he's seen something fascinating, but these males have seen my behind a million times. I can't imagine what's changed, but then again, they've seemed different to me lately as well, with my body responding to them in a way it hasn't in the past.

As I watch their rapt expressions with intrigue, Venom clears his throat and our gazes collide. His pure black eyes squint in amusement, and I give him a cheeky wink before moving on with my yoga pose, swinging one leg forward, my head up and chest out, focusing on my breathing once more. Venom's chuckle behind me is unmistakable.

It's easy for me to forget that they're all technically the predators, and I, their prey. In the beginning, from as early as I can remember, Baabaa, Kit, and I were always separated from the predators of the Ark. As the only true prey in here, there was always an underlying threat of harm that we felt hovering over us, but when we were fourteen, everything changed. That day will forever be tattooed in my mind as one of the worst, and yet, most life-altering days of my existence.

My chest tightens at the memory, and I give my head a small shake, not wanting to relive the moment that my childhood friends were viciously taken from me.

"Don't let it overtake you, Faun," Sabre tells me softly to my right, having approached me soundlessly while I was in my own head. "We won't let anything happen to you."

His large claw-tipped hand tucks a stray lock of my long golden hair behind my ear, and I look over at him with a shaky smile, glad for his comfort. These males are my whole world, and I couldn't imagine one second of my life without them now. The last five years have brought us incredibly close, especially with one of them always with me, to protect me from the other Broken. I owe my life to them.

Sabre is a Broken tiger, and his giant saber teeth earned him his name. All of us have been named from our inner beast in one way or another by the Australian scientist, Dr. Micheals, who is the head scientist of this facility—a facility we've never left. Dr. Adina, the father of the Adina duo, told me it was because he has a terrible sense of humor. I still don't get why one of my dear friends Steve has a human name. He's a Broken Crocodile. Apparently, it's Dr. Micheals' favorite joke, but Steve hates it, insisting that we all call him Crush. But of course, we don't because it's so funny getting a rise out of him.

"I'm alright," I tell Sabre softly. "Thank you."

He smiles widely at me, his sharp teeth on full display. "You're more than welcome, beautiful girl," he tells me openly, and a heated caress touches my cheek at his captivating gaze. Sometimes it feels like there are magnets inside us, drawing me into his soul, and it's not just like that with Sabre, but all the males of my pack.

"I thought you were doing yoga, not listening to this airhead?" Mayne, my Broken lion, growls out, approaching us gruffly.

Mayne and Sabre are the only two of our little group of ten that don't necessarily get along. I like to joke that it's because they're both pussies, but really it's just because they kind of share the title of leader amongst us, and neither of them like that.

I stand up and straighten my body out with a stretch that pushes my chest out, and I notice that both males look briefly at my chest. I don't have massive breasts, but they're still a decent size, so I can't blame them for looking. I would too.

"Do I smell jealousy, Mayne?" Sabre snarks back, and they both narrow their eyes at each other, tensing their sizable shoulders in underlying aggression.

I huff out a breath in frustration and stand between them, slapping a hand to both of their rock-hard chests. "Cut it out, kitty cats, or I'll be forced to put toads in your beds and slugs in your shoes like last time," I threaten playfully. "How about instead of posturing like fools, we go and grab some breakfast before the hall gets too full, and we miss all the good stuff?"

A slimy hiss sounds behind me, and I instantly tense, knowing who's at my back. My instinct to run away almost takes over, but I internally tell myself that I'm safe where I am.

Turning around to face Adda, I plant on a fake smile, which is frankly a waste of time because she can undoubtedly taste my fear. "What do you want, snake?" I ask with way more confidence than I feel.

She snickers creepily, her little fangs peeking out over her thin lips. "I jussst think it'sss hilariousss that you're talking about breakfassst with them when you're meant to be *their* meal." Adda takes a step forward, but both males by my side close their bodies in front of me, effectively blocking me from her view. "Ssssuch a wassste of a good meal, if you asssk me."

"We didn't ask you, so fuck off before I make you into my breakfast," Mayne growls low, but we all know it's not that easy. Unlike Fang, the Broken python, Adda, is extremely venomous and can kill anyone in here in a matter of minutes.

With a freaky hiss that torments my dreams, she turns and leaves, and I let out a shaky breath I didn't realize I was holding. "I hate her," I all but whisper; but with our enhanced senses, I know they can hear me just fine.

"I know," Tallon answers from close behind me. "Me too." His arms wrap me up in a tight hug from behind, and I lean my head back against him with a sigh. If anyone has had a worse time here than me, it's him, and yet he's the reason I have the family that I do.

FIVE YEARS AGO

"That one looks like a turtle," Kit says enthusiastically, pointing up at the fluffy clouds that are holding all of our attention. "Don't you think?"

He smiles at Baabaa and me, his big Beaver teeth sparkling in the light of the sun because of how much he cleans them.

Baabaa scoffs and pushes his hand down. "No way, buddy, that's more like a hippo. You need to put your glasses on. It's no fun playing if you can't see properly." Her shrill voice has me wrinkling my nose.

"Not so loud, your mouth is right near my ear, and you know my hearing is extra strong," I complain, feeling a small headache growing. It doesn't take much to give me one. I try to block out the sounds around me as often as I can so I don't have to deal with it, but it's kind of difficult to avoid *that*.

Baabaa's hands fly to her sheep-like mouth in regret. "Sorry Faun, I forgot," she practically whispers in apology.

"Well, well, well. If it isn't dinner," a deep baritone voice says with a snicker, and we all jolt upright to see Sylva and his troop approaching us with confident strides. I immediately stand up, my fight or flight system kicking into high gear, and its overriding function is always flight. "I could really go for some lamb shanks right about now," Sylva adds on, making the other Broken behind him laugh maliciously.

I don't like the way he's looking at Baabaa because I have no doubt that one of these days, he's going to act on one of his many threats. Turning to the guards patrolling nearby, my hopes are dashed when I hear one of them tell the other that it's about time they got rid of us, before walking away laughing.

The size difference between us and the predators has become really extreme in the last two years; somehow they've almost doubled in size, whereas my friends and I are still petite and fragile looking. I have quite long legs for my height though, and I'm exceptionally fast, but if I run now, I'll be leaving my friends to fend for themselves, and I would never do that. If we go down, we go down together.

Kit grabs my hands and pulls me behind him with Baabaa; and I know he's trying to be sweet, but it's still futile.

"We don't want any trouble," Kit stammers nervously, and I can't help but notice that the courtyard is getting emptier by the second, everyone leaving us to our fate. "We're just gonna go back inside, okay?" Kit finishes, pulling on both of our hands as he tries to walk around them.

Suddenly, Sylva reaches out, clasping his hand around Baabaa's neck and ripping her from Kit's grasp. Quicker than I can follow, Fang steps forward and wraps his long arms around Kit and squeezes so hard that a tiny cry of pain squeaks out of him.

I stand there shocked for a minute, unsure of what to do, while the group laughs and hurts my friends. Mustering all of my courage, I pull on Sylva's arm, trying to get him to let Baabaa go, but he doesn't budge one inch.

Looking down at my friend with a sinister smile, he passes

Baabaa over to King effortlessly, her body dangling off the ground as she fights for breath. King takes her and spins her to face me, her back to his front so she can't see the malicious intent all over his face.

"So, you think you can take me on, little doe?" Sylva asks as he steps up to me, his massive gorilla-like body blocking out the sun as he leans in. "Yet you reek of fear so strong that I can smell your piss. Go on, then, and do your worst."

My legs start shaking uncontrollably, and my mouth is as dry as the Sahara desert, but I look back at my friends and decide *fuck it* and reach up, punching him square in his squished nose. *It was a mistake that I can never take back.*

With a guttural ape call, Sylva rips me up by my wrist as I try to pull it away, and I let loose a piercing scream as I feel the bones in my wrist snap and crumble in his behemoth hand. His movement is so violent that the bone protrudes from my skin and blood pours from the wound.

"Kill them both." Words that will play on a loop for the rest of my life bellow from Sylva, changing my life as I know it.

Baabaa screams, "No!" before Adda strikes her hard on the neck as King restrains her, pumping a lethal amount of venom into her until she starts to convulse right in front of me, her little body shaking wildly.

Sylva grabs my other hand and starts to pull them in opposite directions as if he will tear me in two, and the pain of it has me screaming incoherently, black dots littering my vision as I try not to pass out from the agony.

A choking sound pulls my attention just in time to see Fang crushing the life from Kit while laughing, and the cracking and popping of his bones when his lifeless head lolls are more than I can bear.

Vomit flies from my mouth onto Adda's feet, and Sylva drops me with disgust. My trembling, sobbing body is no more than a heap on the floor. My eyes are tightly closed, but all I can see is my friends' lifeless bodies dangling before me. I vomit again and just before I pass out from shock, Tallon, the Broken Owl, hovers over me with his large eyes wide and... angry?

CHAPTER 2
MAYNE

Turning to Faun, I can tell straight away that her mind has gone back to the fateful day when she became one of us, and I cringe at my own memory of her delicate little body, broken and filthy at Sylva's feet.

I never in a million years would have pictured this female in our lives the way she is, and I certainly couldn't imagine loving her the way I do—the way we all do. Yet, here she is, the center of our world and our biggest weakness.

I'll never forget the way Tallon's head twisted at the sound of her terrified, pain-filled scream. His feet were running toward the courtyard faster than I'd ever seen him move.

It's a rough world that we live in, and we normally keep to our own pack and do not interfere with business that isn't our own. But Tallon had been secretly watching over Faun since the time she helped to nurture him after the guards ripped the wings from his body when he was merely six. So the moment she screamed, we knew she had just become our responsibility. It's the least we could do for the tiny girl that brought a smile back to Tallon's face.

What we weren't prepared for was the stunning beauty that she'd turn into, or more recently, the arousing scent she would start to give off every time she came near one of us.

"Faun?" I gently say, placing my hands gingerly on the sides of her face. "Come on, beautiful, don't think about it."

Easier said than done, I'm sure, but I can't handle that haunted look she gets when those memories relive in her heart, and I have to do something. Her exquisite eyes look up at me, glassy and filled with trust that somehow I'm going to make this world a better, safer place for her, and it damn near brings me to my knees.

I get lost in her soft features, the gentle parting of her lips calling me to taste her, and the erratic beating of her own heart letting me know she wants me as well. Her scent doubles, and Tallon groans behind her, nuzzling the hair at her nape and tightening his grip.

Shit. We're both going to lose our control soon if we don't step away from her. The pheromones she's sending out are strong, like a drug that you can't say no to, and it was hard to stay away from her before that started. But it's our duty to protect her, even if it's from us.

Needing to cut the tension, I take a big step back and say, "You'd better go shower because all that exercise has left you smelling a little extra." I put my hand over my nose to emphasize it. I know it's a low blow, but I also know it'll work because Faun is obsessed with cleanliness.

Right on cue, her sun-kissed cheeks redden with embarrassment, and she all but throws off Tallon's arm from around her, striding off toward the bathroom muttering about me being a dickhead, and I can't contain the deep chuckle that slips out.

Sabre smacks the back of my head. "Seriously, man, that was just mean," he grumbles before chasing after her.

We have a pact between us that none of us will risk our predator side around her by getting too close, in case we hurt her, and that one of us is with her at all times to protect her from others. It works... most of the time. It's getting a fuck load harder to stay away from her, though.

FAUN

After this morning's weird start, everything seemed to go back to normal with the guys. Styng and I played some chess, and the other guys watched some violent movie on Netflix. Apparently, it was awesome, based on the hooting and hollering going on.

Now I'm just sitting on the sidelines watching them play football, with Tallon as the referee, because running around really isn't his favorite thing to do.

Nanuk, Sabre, Venom, and Steve are the shirtless team, and lord have mercy, it's by far my favorite idea of a uniform. The sweaty eight packs and gleaming back muscles have got me feeling all sorts of things I know I shouldn't be.

The other team, which unfortunately are fully clothed, are Ironside, Mayne, Styng, and Alfa.

I don't really understand this game, but the guys seem to really enjoy it, even though it's super violent. Or more likely *because* it's violent.

Ironside smashes the funny-shaped ball on the ground and starts running around whooping. He suddenly turns and bolts toward me, making me jump up from my seat with a squeal. I spin and start to run, knowing he's gunning for me, but I didn't react fast enough.

My body gets flung into the air and twisted so that I land with a thud on his gigantic shoulder, my head bouncing off his back as he runs back to the oval, laughing playfully.

"I am the winner, and I happily claim my prize. This fair maiden will do nicely," Ironside announces in a booming voice, and I giggle when I hear a few growls from the others.

Slap.

His hand comes down on my ass unexpectedly, and I don't hate it. If anything, it makes my insides clench and my core tighten. I jolt as we stop suddenly, and the hand holding my legs to his chest tightens.

"What's wrong?" I ask, tapping his butt softly.

Ironside is a Broken rhinoceros and the skin all over his body is the same as the real thing: tough, strong, and gray. His butt is as hard as a rock under my hands, and I give it another tap for good measure.

Slap.

He whacks my ass again without replying to me, and I squirm a little as tingles flick over my pussy. I push out a breath and ask him what he's doing, but he doesn't answer me again, instead slapping my ass one more time, only a bit harder than before.

A moan slips free, and I'm stunned at Nanuk barking at Ironside, "Put her down."

The only response from him is a grunt before he steps back, away from the others.

"What's going on, big guy?" I ask, wiggling to try and see what's happening. "I can't see."

"Ironside," Alfa, the sweetest of the group, says quietly. "You need to focus and put her down now, or you're going to hurt her. Look at how small she is, then look at you, mate. Big difference, yeah?"

I giggle. "Don't be silly, Alfa, he won't hurt me." He may be the biggest, but he's always super gentle with me. Granted, the butt slaps are new, but I kind of enjoyed that, so I don't think it counts.

Ironside grunts and says in a surprisingly husky voice, "Of course not," before pulling me up and sliding my body down his slowly. Torturously slow. When my front slides down a noticeably large bulge, my cheeks flush, and I look up at him to see his gaze hooded and solely on me.

His nose twitches as he clearly scents me, and his eyes hood further. My core clenches again, wetness pooling there. I shiver in his bulging arms and lick my suddenly dry lips.

Like I'm on fire, Ironside lets go of me and spins, practically running back inside without a backward glance. Not sure what I did wrong, I turn to the guys behind me and find them all further away than they sounded a minute ago, except Steve, who just stands there smiling at me with a big goofy grin.

"What are you smiling at, Steve?" I ask him, knowing he hates to be called that.

His smile drops and he points to his chest proudly. "My name is Crush now, remember?"

I crinkle my nose at him, smiling, and walk over to tap his chest. "Sure it is, Steve." I get on my tiptoes and kiss his cheek. "Why don't you go and see what's wrong with Ironside?"

He frowns for a split second at my use of his name, but then smiles widely. "I already know what's wrong with him. It's your smell."

My mouth drops open in shock. Why does everyone keep telling me I smell? Before I can berate his bad manners, a shirtless Venom runs over and grabs Steve's arm, pulling him back into the new game they've just started. His smooth black skin glimmers with a sheen of sweat, and the red hourglass marking on his chest that gives away his beast sticks out more than normal, catching my eye.

With a *humph* of frustration, I go back to my previously abandoned seat and sit with a heavy plonk, crossing my arms petulantly. When I notice the guys aren't looking at me, I discreetly sniff both of my armpits, but don't think I smell too bad. Looking back up, I catch Mayne and Styng laughing at me.

Damn, I was caught out. Like the true lady I am, I stick my tongue out and give them the finger, making them laugh harder. *Bastards.*

I wait patiently on the sidelines, periodically looking at the doors that Ironside disappeared into, but he doesn't come back. I quietly wonder if he's embarrassed that I felt his hard manhood against me, because I didn't mind, and from what it felt like he has absolutely nothing to be embarrassed about. In fact, I didn't even know they got that big. That was the most shocking thing about it, except maybe how my own body reacted to feeling him like that.

"It's starting to get dark, precious. Do you want to come inside with me?" Tallon asks me as the group disperses. "We can even watch one of those girly movies you like so much."

"Really?" I ask with surprise because they usually don't like watching my stuff.

He just laughs and grabs my hand, pulling me to my feet and wrapping his hand around my shoulder. "Yes, really. I'll walk you to your room to get into your comfy PJs first, and then we'll snuggle up with some snacks."

My pace picks up in excitement. "Oh, you have snacks? Yay."

We head off, leaving a trail of Tallon's joyous laugh behind us.

CHAPTER 3
FAUN

I suck in a deep breath and jolt upright, sweat covering my face and chest, my hair stuck unceremoniously all over my face, and I don't give a shit. *What was that?*

Flashes of the dream I just had fly through my mind, making me heat up all over again. Images of Steve with his head buried in between my legs, while Alfa licks and nips at my taut nipples, enough to make me shudder and pant. Holy fuck, that was hot.

It sucks hardcore that I woke a second before I came, and by the feel of the pulse in between my legs, I really would have. Lying back down, I spread my legs and reach into my underwear. I feel the slick heat built up there and use the wetness I find to rub soft circles around my clit, surprised by how close I am to finishing with just one touch.

My door thrusts open and Nanuk comes stomping in. "What happened?" he growls with his elongated claws out and ready to go as he scans my room for an intruder. Within seconds he freezes, his dark eyes widening comically as he takes me in, scenting the air. If this white boy could get any whiter, he did.

I instantly feel bad for him, but I'm also equally mortified and pull the blanket up to my nose, trying to hide from the situation.

"I, um, you, um," Nanuk stumbles out awkwardly, and I groan, covering my whole head this time. "Sorry, I didn't realize you did that."

What a stupid fucking thing to say. Pissed off with him now, I grumble out, "Go away."

"For what it's worth, it's a totally natural thing to do. In fact, I was doing the same thing earlier," he continues, trying to be helpful, but in reality, he's digging himself deeper into a hole.

I jump out of bed and run at him. His eyes go wide again and his hands drop by his side in shock. As I reach him, he grabs my shoulders as if he's going to pull me in, but I shove at his chest. To no avail, of course, because he's a freaking polar bear splice.

"Out Nanuk. You've said quite enough," I practically yell at him, embarrassment filling me at being caught.

He lets me go and steps back, rubbing his head in confusion. "You don't want to cuddle or something?" he asks with a befuddled expression. "You smell very strong."

"Are you fucking kidding me right now? Get. Out."

Reluctantly, he leaves the room, looking back at me as he closes the door like he's waiting for me to change my mind. At this rate, I'm going to get a complex and shower five times a day.

I return to the bed, feeling resigned and slightly defeated. *I think something is wrong with me.* I'm constantly hot and sweating even though it's October, my hormones are all over the place, and the guys keep insisting that I stink.

Right, I'll go see Dr. Adina tomorrow and see what she says. She's always been the closest human to me here, other than her father. I'm sure she'll get to the bottom of it.

I RELEASE a nervous breath and approach the guard at the door that separates us from the rest of the world.

We may be in a compound designed to box us in forever, but we've never been sheltered from what the rest of the human race is like. We have access to television, radio stations, and an array of things that remind us of everything we're missing out on. The only thing we don't have access to is any way of contacting anyone outside these walls.

In order to see Dr. Adina, I have to get through the guard, Antonio, first, and he makes it his mission to punish us whenever he can. The enjoyment he feels at our pain and screams is written all over his smug face, and I usually do everything I can to keep my distance from him.

Antonio looks over at me as I cautiously approach him, and I have to fight every fiber of my being, telling me to turn around and run away. My instincts have always been strong when it comes to who's friend and who's foe.

"Looky here guys, venison's come for a visit," Antonio crows with a smirk. *Really original douche bag.*

I look down submissively, knowing that's what he expects from me. "Sorry, sir, but may I please go through to see Dr. Adina? I'm having some health issues." I make sure to say it loud enough for him to hear but soft enough that he can't say that I'm giving him any attitude.

Antonio beat it into us from a very young age the way he expects us to behave; and while I'm happy to do whatever will keep the peace, the Broken predators have a much harder time bowing down to a 'mere' human.

Humming under his breath in a way that indicates he's pleased with my response to his authority, he says, "Alright, follow me. You know the rules."

I sure do. We all do. I eye his cattle prod as I recite them in my head. *Keep silent and only speak when spoken to. Don't stray. No sudden movements. Be submissive. Keep one meter between the guard in front and behind. Do exactly what you're told, immediately.* Any deviation from the rules results in a severe beating and two weeks in complete isolation, with only one cup of water and one bread roll a day.

As we walk silently down the glistening white hall lined with glaring fluorescent lights, the overwhelming scent of chemicals makes my nose twitch in discomfort, but I don't dare to make a move to rub it.

Antonio knocks three times harder than necessary on Dr. Adina's door, and when it opens wide, his goofy smile at the pretty doctor gives away the crush he has on her. It's been obvious since she first started working here eight years ago, but what is equally obvious is her distaste for the man. It takes all of my will not to giggle when I see her roll her eyes at him and look past his dopey face to smile at me, making no effort to acknowledge the guard past that.

"Faun. How are you? Come in, come in," she says excitedly. "I was wondering if you were going to pop by and see me soon."

Antonio clears his voice, hardening his face as he sneers down at me, angry that I took attention away from him. "This is an official meeting, Dr. Adina, not a social club. This Broken is ill and needs medical care."

Pushing Antonio out of the way, Dr. Adina steps up to me, looking at me from head to toe with a worried expression. "Oh dear, what's happened? Has somebody hurt you?" Her concern for me warms my heart, as always, and I'm once again grateful that she works here.

"I'm fine, honestly. There's just been a few things worrying me, and I wondered if I could ask you about them?" I ask, side-eyeing the guard because I really don't want to get into it while he's standing over me.

Dr. Adina gets the hint and grabs my hand softly, ushering me inside the room, but before the door closes, Antonio stops it with his heavy booted foot and squeezes himself inside, closing the door and leaning against it with his arms folded over his chest.

"What exactly do you think you're doing, Antonio?" Dr. Adina snaps at him while pushing me gently into the seat across from where she normally sits. Her office is quite big, with a hospital bed set up to the left, her desk to the right, and two comfortable armchairs in the center, which is where we usually spend the time here.

I sit down quickly, knowing by the look on her face to stay out of it and be quiet, and true to my observation, Dr. Adina's face changes to a sweet soft one as she smiles at him. It's obviously fake to anyone that has half a brain, but luckily for us, he doesn't.

"Antonio, I know that you're trying to protect me and I appreciate that. However, we are going to be talking about periods and all that yucky stuff. I'm just trying to save you from being in an uncomfortable situation." She shrugs in innocence and Antonio's face looks disgusted, yet undecided. So Dr. Adina says, as I desperately try not to laugh, "All that blood and yucky mucus. It's all just so messy."

Antonio's face pales, and he looks a little queasy as he puts his hand up in defense. "You know, I think I will stay out there. Just call me if you need anything." He leaves the room so fast that he almost forgets his shadow, and as the door closes behind him, we both silently shake in laughter at his predictability.

"Thank you for seeing me, Dr. Adina. I know you're really busy," I say gratefully as she sits across from me.

She waves her hand and tells me, "Please Faun, call me Morigan. We've known each other long enough it seems silly that you don't. Only in private, of course. I'd hate to get you into any trouble. I know buffoons like Antonio look for any excuse to punish you."

We both know that it's not just because I'm Broken, but also because I'm the only remaining prey. It's not just the predators that I need to be careful of; the humans that work here have made it very clear that they think my creation was a mistake they'd like to rectify.

"Are you sure?" I question, secretly loving that she wants me to call her by her name. I try to keep my eagerness hidden, but a relieved exhale leaves me when she insists.

"Now tell me, what brings you in to see me today? You seem a bit more nervous than usual?" Morigan asks me.

I carefully explain how I've been feeling lately and the changes that my body has been going through, as well as how my pack has been treating me differently. How they're either keeping me at arm's length like they can't stand being near me, or they stare at me like I hold all the answers of the universe. I finish with my apparently terrible smell that I myself don't notice.

Morigan listens attentively, nodding occasionally, but otherwise silent. When I finish with my explanation, we both just sit there without a sound between us, me because of my confusion and her with eyes filled with obvious scientific curiosity about my evolved situation. I can practically see her mind ticking away at all the possibilities.

"Do you think this is normal?" I question, unable to take the silence anymore.

A laugh ripples from Morigan, and she crosses her legs, leaning back in the chair comfortably. "Faun, you are the very first of your kind. I have no idea. However, I will do a little research and see what I can find out. I wouldn't stress too much. None of what you've told me sounds alarming at all, and I personally don't think you smell, but my sniffer isn't quite the same as your friends."

She pinches her chin in thought before saying, "And as for the way the males are treating you, well, have you seen yourself?" Morigan waves her hand in my direction. "You're stunning. I'm sure they're just trying to figure out how to get into your pants."

My cheeks instantly redden, and my mind flicks back to my earlier dream and how good it felt to touch myself afterward.

"Ah, I see." Morigan puts her foot back down and leans forward with a cheeky look in her eyes. "You wouldn't mind that one bit, would you? If you don't mind me asking, have you had much experience with the males like that? Not that you have anything to worry about because you're all of clean health, and with your shot, you can't fall pregnant."

I shake my head slowly. "It's never been like that before, but lately, I've been seeing them differently."

"That much I *can* say is normal," Morigan tells me, smiling. "Which guy has caught your eye?"

My head cocks to the side. "Um, all of them. Was I only meant to want one of them?"

Morigan clears her throat and smiles wider, telling me cryptically, "Not if you ask some of my favorite authors." She suddenly claps her hands together and says, "Honestly, if I were to hazard a guess, I would say that you're coming into your first heat. Some of the other girls have gone through it, but most of their splices don't require a heat cycle. You, however, are part deer, and usually, they go into heat from October until December. Which may mean that this is just the beginning, and your symptoms could get a lot worse before they get better. If it continues to increase, I'd like you to come back, and we can talk about alternative ways of dealing with it, other than the obvious way if you're not ready for that route yet. For now, though, I'll take some blood samples and get you to pee in a cup for me. I'll do a few tests in case it's something else. How does that sound?"

I nod and ask, slightly confused, "What is the *obvious route?*"

"Sex, Faun. The obvious route is sex." Her bluntness surprises me, but I did ask.

At my heated cheeks, I can see her try to cover her amusement with her hand and I stand, excusing myself. Morigan reminds me that I'm welcome any time, even if I just want someone to talk to, before getting Antonio to escort me back.

As I follow him down the long hallway, I wonder if she's right. Is all I need to feel better sex? Can it really be that simple? But even if I do decide to try that, who would I ask? How could I ever be expected to choose in my pack when I want them all equally?

CHAPTER 4
SABRE

THE WORLD DRIFTS AWAY LIKE IT USUALLY DOES AS I WATCH Faun glide across the dining hall, a soft smile on her lips as she chats animatedly with Ironside.

Her natural beauty is unmatched in every way, and each time I lay eyes on her, it's as if I can't breathe. Lately, when I remember to inhale again, all I can smell and taste is her. Her want and need, her scent that makes my mouth salivate to taste her, and not in the way a tiger normally tastes a deer. I dream of devouring her core. Of licking every inch of it until she screams for me.

I have no idea what changed in Faun, but it's harder now than it ever has been to stay away from her. I let the tip of my tongue tap against my protruding tooth as a reminder of how much of a threat I am to her, and how I can never be trusted anywhere near her most vulnerable area. I could never live with myself if I hurt her in some way.

My previously raging hard-on instantly deflates at the idea of her in any kind of pain.

Mayne is right, even though I'll never say that out loud. Faun must be protected at all costs because we can't trust our beast side around her. What if we lost control in the heat of the moment? No. I will never let it even become a possibility.

I barely tolerate that stupid feline as it is, but when it comes to our female, we always agree, and she is *our* female. I would have to be an idiot to think that she could ever be just mine. We are a pack, and we share everything equally, including our love and need for this beautiful little creature that came into our lives and ripped open our hearts with her scream.

We've never looked back since that dreadful day, and we never will. The nights we laid by her bed as she thrashed in her nightmares, the days we pleaded for her to eat again, and the tears that soaked our chests as she grieved; they all cemented her to us forever, tattooing her life with ours... And I wouldn't change a thing.

Even if I can never have her the way that my body craves, there's nothing in this world that could make me leave her side, and I could never be with any of the other harpies in this place.

Nope. Faun is the only female for me.

"What are you thinking about?" Her angelic voice snaps me back into reality, as she slides into the seat next to me with her hand near my mouth, holding a piece of marinated meat out for me.

I lean forward and take it from her fingers carefully so that my two large teeth don't touch her fragile digits. She pushes it in a bit deeper and softly touches the tip of my tongue. I instantly close my lips around her finger and suck off the juice, while gazing deep into her gray eyes.

Faun shudders and pulls it back slowly, still not taking her eyes from mine, and it takes every bit of my willpower not to pull her into my lap and kiss her stupid. Instead, I answer simply, "How hungry I am."

Ironside barks out a laugh from the other side of her, saying in understanding, "Aren't we all brother, aren't we all?"

Not understanding my double meaning, she crinkles her golden nose and lifts her fork with some salad, rolling her eyes and shaking her head. "Well, eat then."

I freaking wish.

FAUN

Waking up saturated in sweat from another sexy as fuck dream — this time about Venom fucking me hard from behind — I curse under my breath because I felt so close to a happy ending before life came crashing back.

There's no way I'm going to touch myself right now, not after last time. Closing my eyes, I try to think of something else, but the memory of him thrusting inside me has them snapping right back open again.

Why is it so fucking hot in here?

I kick my sheets off and swing my legs off the bed, sitting on the edge. I thread my long fingers through my hair and rub at my antlers soothingly, trying to shake off the thrumming between my thighs.

I wonder if the others would enjoy watching something like that? I bet it would feel great to have their hooded eyes on me as I cum.

"Agh." I stand up, frustrated at my unhelpful thoughts, and start to pace the room in frustration, my skin on fire and my loins burning for something that I don't fully understand.

While I know what sex is because I've seen it enough on TV to know what it all means, I can't really imagine what it would be like. Is it really as good as it sounds, or is it just skin moving against skin?

I'm so curious and really want to try it, but can't imagine just being like, "Hey, can one of you have sex with me?" I shake my head at the ludicrous idea. There's no way I'd ever be brave enough to do that. Or could I?

Even if I could summon up enough courage to ask for what haunts me in my very vivid dreams, how could I ask one over another? Would the others be pissed off that I didn't ask them? Or would the male I ask be grossed out and deny me? Or worse, say yes out of pity?

This sucks.

Deciding that I've had enough of torturing myself with pointless thoughts, I grab new pajamas out of my drawer and leave the room, determined that I need to wash off all the sweat and dirty ideas.

I know it's against the guy's rules that I walk around unsupervised at night, but I can't stay cooped up right now, and I no doubt stink again. I'm sure I'll be fine.

Just to be safe, I focus on my senses as I look down the hall, but I can't hear anyone else; and my nose doesn't pick up any strong scents indicating that someone has been near this area in a while.

Shrugging, I close my door and head toward the female bathroom around the next corner, keeping my eyes trained on the shadows, and my ears perked up for any new sounds.

I turn the bend but find no one in between me and the doorway I'm after. Picking up my steps, I quickly enter the shared bathroom, my heart thumping harder than I'd like to admit, considering I only just went around the corner.

Closing my eyes, I lean against the wall and catch my breath while telling my heart to slow down and that I'm safe; but of course, I'm just not lucky enough for that to be the truth.

I freeze as my hearing picks up a slow heartbeat approaching me from the other end of the room, and I snap my eyes open just in time to find Adda closing me in with her body against the wall behind me.

Her smile is as cruel as her eyes are excited, telling me the story of my immediate fate. The fate she's been trying to dish to me for so many years, and my own stupidity gifted my ass to her on a silver platter.

I exhale shakily as Adda's long forked tongue flicks against my cheek, her tightly slicked back short hair making her seem even more reptilian this close up.

"It'sss sssuch a tragedy that you forgot your guard dogsss tonight," she hisses at me in a pleased tone. "I guess they'll have to misss the show."

I freeze in fear as she cackles maliciously, lowering her mouth to my neck, but before her fangs can pierce my skin, effectively killing me, Ironside tackles her to the ground, with Venom hot on his heels.

Ironside holds down her flailing body as Venom grabs Adda's head in his vice grip. "Move again, bitch, and the only person dying from poison tonight is you." To make his point clear, his own fangs appear, dripping with his just as potent venom.

Still unable to move because of the adrenaline and fear racing through me at my near death, a small squeak leaves me as a large hand lands on my shoulder.

"It's okay, pretty girl, it's just me. You're safe now," Nanuk says soothingly, standing in front of me and leaning down so that I can take in his worried features. "Didn't we tell you not to go wandering off at night?" His voice is filled with concern.

I let myself relax and step forward into his waiting arms, letting him surround me completely, the giant size of his body making me feel tiny but utterly safe within his grasp.

"I'm sorry." My words tumble out of my trembling lips weakly.

Without another word, Nanuk picks me up like I weigh nothing and carries me out of the room, leaving the scene of what's happening with the others behind us.

Instead of taking me back to my room, Nanuk takes me back to his. I don't complain because I don't want to be alone right now. He places me carefully down onto his much larger bed and goes to close the door, turning the light off before returning to my side.

I wiggle myself under his blankets and move over for him. But when he gets under the blanket with me, he slides down the bed, placing a heavy arm around my waist, before resting his head on my chest, right above my heart.

"I was scared I was going to lose you," he mumbles against me, his hot breath tickling my sensitive skin. "Don't ever frighten me like that again, pretty girl. Please."

Speechless from his honest declaration and lingering terror from what just happened, I don't reply. Instead, I bring one arm around his back and stroke his hair gently off his face in soothing motions, grateful that he's with me and that these men made it in time to save me again.

I focus on the feeling of his soft locks against my fingertips and the warm air trailing across me—instead of thinking about Adda—and start to hum a gentle tune, letting the darkness swallow us both until we're relaxed again in each other's arms. My tune slowly trails off as sleep claims me, and my last thoughts are of how I've never felt safer than I am right now.

CHAPTER 5
NANUK

ABSOLUTELY CAPTIVATED, I WATCH FAUN'S CHEST RISE AND FALL with each relaxed breath, her perfect lips slightly parted as she sleeps deeply. She is the epitome of sleeping beauty, with her delicate features and peaceful state of rest. I find myself torn on whether to let her sleep like this all day and enjoy the first time I've ever really seen her so at ease, or to lean down and take her plump lips with mine, tasting her innocence and keeping it forever.

My choice is taken away from me, luckily, because I find myself unconsciously leaning in as she begins to stir, her long eyelashes fluttering slightly as her face turns away.

I force myself to move back just in time as her eyes open, and she smiles up at me sweetly, her arms going above her head as she arches her back in a languid stretch. The softness to her eyes as she gazes at me has my heart missing a beat. Faun is absolutely everything, and the familiarity we always have together is just another reminder that she belongs with me, with *us*.

"How was your sleep?" I ask, focusing on her needs and not my own, as always.

"Surprisingly good, to be honest," Faun says with a yawn, and reaches up, stroking her hand down my cheek lovingly. The contact feels so warm and right that my eyes close, and I lean into her touch. "All I want is a small sense of normalcy in my life. I hate feeling hunted all the time and scared for my life. Thank you for sleeping with me last night. I needed you."

Her words are heartbreakingly honest, and they rock me to my core. If only she knew how much I also needed it. Feeling her warm body next to mine all night was a dream come true.

A familiar and enticing scent tickles at my nose and my eyes snap open to find Faun's half-lidded, our proximity burning my insides.

"I, ah, might go and take a shower," she says huskily, as she looks at my twitching nose. "I probably stink again and frankly, right now I could really use a cold one."

Fuck. Me too!

Her scent rises with my hitched breath at her confession. The knowledge that she's almost lying under me, and she's as horny as I am, fills me with a sudden need to devour her.

I lower my nose to the nape of her neck and breathe in deeply, my body pressing against hers in a way that I know she can feel how hard I am. My dick feels almost painful as it throbs with the need to claim her as my own.

Faun's heart rate picks up against my lips as I trail them softly back and forth over her exposed neck, and her scent doubles in potency, making my mouth salivate to taste her. To feel her slick heat cover my hungry tongue.

Groaning deeply, I roll my hips up, rubbing myself on her in the process. What I would give to feel her hot skin against mine.

With a quick movement, Faun turns her body toward me, wrapping her hands around the back of my neck and her leg over my hip to grind her pussy over the large bulge in my pants, while pulling my head closer to her neck, practically begging me with her body to do more. And fuck me sideways if I don't want to do just that.

Her tiny, vulnerable frame clings to me, reminding me of our size difference, and reality slams back to me like an icy surge. I squeeze my eyes closed, trying desperately to remember why this is a bad idea, and willing myself to find the strength to leave. *God, I hate myself right now.*

With slow, deliberate movements, I carefully remove her hands from the back of my head and her leg off me. The minute she realizes what I'm doing, her body grows cold and tense.

"I'm sorry," I practically whisper, regret lacing every word, and I pray that she can hear it. "I'm gonna go."

Reluctantly, I slide off the bed and head straight for the door. Too chicken shit to look at her face, scared of what I'll find there. Scared of the hurt that I know I've caused, and I know if I look back at her, I'll change my mind and take her with or without any sense.

I close the door behind me and lean my back on it heavily, bending forward with my elbows on my knees and my hands cupping my face.

I'm such an asshole, but I could never live with myself if I hurt her.

Now I really need that cold shower. I don't know how much longer I'll be able to keep this shit up. The polar bear part of me rears up with need every time I smell her these days, and the worst part is that I can't guarantee I won't accidentally hurt her. It's my worst fear, and I've had more than one nightmare about it that's effectively keeping me from getting proper sleep these days.

I find myself torn because I can't just stay here, outside the bedroom door, without wanting to rip it off its hinges to get back to her. Leaving her alone at any time is too risky.

VENOM

Rounding the corner, I'm surprised to find Nanuk outside his door, looking defeated and, frankly, in pain.

"What's going on, my man?" I ask, concerned about why he's

looking so beaten down, and a rogue thought has my steps quickening as I query, "Is Faun okay? Did something happen?"

It doesn't slip my notice that he breathes out a relieved exhale at my approach, his body instantly relaxing. Which puts me at ease as well because if something was really wrong, there's no way he'd lose his tension so easily.

"Dude, am I glad to see you," he huffs out. "I need to get out of here. This is too much."

Nanuk scrubs his clawed hands back and forth through his thick white hair on his head, the bright hairs on his forearms almost glowing under the fluorescent lights of the clinical hallway.

That's when I take in a deep breath. My sense of smell is nowhere near as effective as most of the others, but it's still above that of a human, and I can't miss the faint scent of Faun's heightened pheromones all over him.

"Ah," I say knowingly, clapping my hand on his massive shoulder. "Did you get too close to the fire, my friend?"

Nanuk snorts a laugh. "You could say that." He pauses, then looks at me hard. "She's changing, and I'm not so sure if I can do this anymore. I was way too close to losing control in there, and she wanted me. She wanted me bad. What should I do?"

I tongue my right fang in contemplation because I've noticed it too. We all have. "I have no idea, and you're not the only one. I think it's time we had a meeting."

"How? Someone needs to watch her," Nanuk grumbles, pointing at the door.

"Do you think she'll come out any time soon?" I ask, and he grimaces, telling me that his departure from the room wasn't smooth.

Shaking his head ruefully, Nanuk says, "I doubt it. It wouldn't surprise me if she's crying at the moment. I left her in a bad way, but I didn't know what to do."

"Shit."

"Yep, shit alright." Nanuk's face contorts with regret, and I feel bad for the guy, but not as much as I feel bad for Faun.

I sigh deeply, knowing that I'm going to have to check on her now. "Go and get the others," I tell him, moving my hand to the doorknob. "Tell them it's important. I'll go and see if she's alright and then meet you at the corner over there because as long as we can see the door, she should be perfectly fine." I gesture in the direction that I just came from.

With a swift nod, Nanuk takes off like his ass is on fire, and I take a deep breath before I turn the handle and step into his room. Straight away, I can tell she hasn't moved from the big bed in the center of the room and the covers are ripped over her head, the tip of her beautiful antlers sticking out the top.

"I heard you," the blankets mumble. "I get it, okay. No one wants me like that. You guys have made that very clear."

I deflate a little, forgetting momentarily that her hearing is excellent. My mind quickly flicks through what we said, but I don't think there was anything too bad, so I walk over to the bed and sit on the edge. "Don't be like that, Faun. Come out of there."

"I'm not crying, and I have no interest in hearing you guys gossiping about how I 'want him bad'," Faun says sadly, the blankets still covering her.

I can see how that sounded bad.

Grabbing the edge of the blanket, I pull it down slowly, revealing her soft face, pink with embarrassment. "It's not what you think, so stop jumping to conclusions. Nanuk was flustered because of whatever happened in here and doesn't want to hurt you."

"Too late," she whispers, looking anywhere but at me. "I feel like an idiot. I thought he wanted me back, but he couldn't get out of here quick enough. He didn't even look back. How am I supposed to feel?"

I tuck a loose strand of her golden hair behind her ear and shake my head at his stupidity. *Real smooth dickhead.* "You know he has no game, Faun. He wouldn't know what charm is if it smacked him in the face. Don't let this bring you down. You're beautiful, smart, and intelligent, and he'd be lucky to have you, but it's not that simple, and you should know that. You're prey and we're not."

The second I say those words, I know I've made a mistake by the flash of hurt in her eyes before she visibly shuts down, hardening her features and sucking in a breath.

"Thanks for clearing that up. You can go and gossip now. They're here." Her words are clipped and angry. *I fucked up.*

Reaching for her hand, I'm not surprised when she pulls her hand from mine immediately, before turning away from me and bringing the blanket back over her head. And honestly, I don't blame her. That came out all wrong. I know how she feels about being prey, and saying what I did probably hurt her more than whatever happened with Nanuk.

A small knock taps on the door before Steve pops his head in and says quietly, "Do you mind if I steal Venom for a minute?"

Faun ignores him and his eyebrows raise at me, but I shake my head and follow him out of the room, looking back as I close the door to find her unmoved.

Steve goes to say something, but I just shake my head again and point to the far corner where the other males are congregated. Getting my hint, he closes his mouth, and we join the others quietly.

"We need to whisper because she heard me and Nanuk earlier and is pissed about it," I warn in a low voice, noticing Nanuk cringe.

Without hesitation, Nanuk quietly explains what happened between them and how he's at his wit's end with the whole thing, because the temptation that is *Faun* is too much to handle now.

"I'd like to propose an idea," Sabre starts. "Why don't we kick up her security detail to us doing it in groups of two now instead of by ourselves? It should help us control ourselves better if we have another person to pull us up if we start to stray from the pact. I've got to be honest, I'm really hesitant at this point to be left alone with her because the tiger in me is getting feisty as fuck every time I'm anywhere near her."

I agree wholeheartedly, and so do the others.

"What do we tell Faun when she notices what is happening?" Styng asks, worried about how it's going to negatively affect her.

Alfa scoffs, "Tell her the truth: it's for her own safety." His face is as somber as I feel when he says that, because it is the truth; none of us would be putting ourselves through the hell of denying ourselves—or her—if we didn't truly believe that we were a safety risk. "And it's important that none of us lose sight of that, not for a moment."

CHAPTER 6
FAUN

"THE GUYS ARE MORE DISTANT THAN NORMAL, AND I HATE IT," I tell Morigan with a frustrated whine. "The needier I seem to be, the further away they seem to get from me, and I don't know what to do."

Morigan pulls on her earring and puffs out a breath. "It's surprising that they're acting that way. I've seen the way they look at you, and with you coming into full-blown heat now, I would've thought they'd be clamoring for affection by now."

Coming in to see her today, I was glad to find out that there was nothing wrong with me beyond going into heat, but it doesn't really help my situation any. Every day, it hurts more and more, and the ache I'm feeling is getting intolerable.

"What do I do?"

She pops her lips and crosses her arms, deep in thought, before saying. "Honestly, this should get a whole lot worse before it gets better if you don't find someone to help you through it. I know that it's a lot for you to take in because you've never done stuff like that before; but in my medical opinion, I think you need to decide which one of them you trust to be by your side through this. I'm sure if you sit them down and tell them what's going on and how hard this is for you to deal with alone, they'll help you in a safe and understanding way. Your pack is filled with the kindest men in here by far, and I can't imagine any of them wanting you to be in pain. But as a friend, I can understand that it's not that easy to open up to them like that and put yourself in such a vulnerable situation."

"That's exactly it. We're such a close group. What if me asking for something so intimate changes the dynamic, or they see it as just another weakness?" I respond honestly, my chest tight at the thought of pushing them away. "I couldn't bear losing them."

"I don't think you're giving them enough credit, Faun. They've always been there for you and each other. I don't think this situation will be any different," Morigan says as she grabs me a glass of water, passing it to me with a look too close to pity for my liking. "Plus, you never know. You might just find yourself a permanent partner out of one of them. Someone that you can spend your life with and learn to love in a whole different way."

The problem with that is that I already love them in a way that I know I shouldn't, and it only grows every year that we get to spend together. My second problem is that I love them all equally. How could I devote myself to one of them while hiding my feelings for the others? It doesn't seem right.

Instead of telling her that, I just nod and sip the crisp cold water, and focus on the refreshing way it slides down my throat. While it doesn't feel wrong, I'm not so sure that the guys will feel the same way.

"So, what *are* you gonna do?" she asks, curiosity brimming in her eyes. "If you were to pick one of them to ask, who would it be?"

I think about each one of them and the different things that they bring to my life. Mayne, with his strong, unyielding support and constant demand to protect me. Sabre with his piercing eyes that seem to notice even the slightest of needs that I have. Nanuk with his clueless but sweet companionship. Tallon with his gigantic heart and courage. Venom with his knowing comfort and guidance. Steve, with his dirty mind and ability to always make me happy. Alfa and his loyalty and devotion that stem from a never-ending stream of kindness; he doesn't have an overly huge personality, but he's always genuine. Styng who never lets me down and always has a terrible dad joke ready to make me smile. And Ironside, the giant male that's as big as he is soft.

How could I ever pick one to trust over the other? Which arms should I want to hold me? Who will I willingly give my innocence to over the other eight?

"I have no idea!"

My calculating gaze rolls over the enticing specimens before me, like a smorgasbord for the senses as they play pool together. I take in their hard bodies, angular faces, Broken features, and watch the way they move around the room with a fluidity that a human would never possess.

I purposely inhale each of their individual aromas, bathing in the way they grow and dip between them, focusing on the moments when potent arousal spikes through them when I cross my bare legs; the short skirt I chose to wear today helping to sway them in my favor.

For today, unbeknownst to them, I am the predator, and they're my prey. I woke up today with my inner goddess in charge and ready to mate, and I'm no longer willing to let them sidestep me. Now it's up to me to decide on which one of these enticing males I'm going to feast on.

Ironside catches my gaze and I smile seductively at him, and I get up from my seat, swaying my hips as I approach him sitting on the arm of a chair opposite me.

Pride fills me as I notice his Adam's apple bobbing nervously as he swallows, and I lick my lips, sliding in between his legs so that my face is only inches from him; and I gently rub my hands from his knees up to his thighs.

His hands clench the navy material of the armchair, but other than that, he stays completely still. I feel emboldened by his lack of disagreement and lean into him, letting my breasts rub against his wide chest, my nipples instantly hardening at the contact, and I barely manage to suppress a moan.

"Um, Faun, it's your turn," Mayne says from right behind me, his body heat licking at my back.

Spinning around, I move into him before he gets a chance to move away and slide my arms around his neck, under his wild mane of hair, and pull myself close. I'm rewarded with a shocked gasp and a hard bulge pressing into my stomach.

I smile sweetly up at him and bite my lip before thanking him, and I slide my body along his as I let go and turn toward the pool table and the frozen males surrounding it.

In two steps, I make it to Sabre's almost vibrating body. The lust rolling off him is an excellent indication that Operation Seduction is working. Instead of just grabbing the offered pool cue from him, the tip of my finger strokes one of his large protruding teeth, then over his slightly parted lips. Letting it drop to his chest, I watch my hand with renewed fascination as it explores his solid pecs and down over his bulging bicep until I all but tangle my fingers with his over the long stick that he now has in a death grip.

Flicking my eyes back to his, desire coats my core at the heated look of his primal gaze. "Can I have your stick?" I rasp, the heat in me rising dangerously.

The silence in the room is almost deafening in its ferocity. The only sound is the background noise from the compound beyond this room.

"Holy shit, bro, give her the cue before I empty my manhood in my pants," Steve moans, breaking Sabre's intensity, and he promptly lets it go, stepping away from me as if out of everybody here, *I* was the big bad.

The thought almost makes me chuckle, but I hold it in and instead turn toward the table, winking at Steve as I pass him and stop beside Styng.

"Can you show me how to do this again?" I ask him, turning my back to him and bending over the table in a position that shows that I want to play, but with my ass lined up with his crotch like I saw on TV once.

When he doesn't answer, I look back over my shoulder at him, my eyes heavy with seduction. His signature stinger waves behind him in a dance as he stares longingly at my position, and as his gaze roams my body, landing on my own, I feel my underwear dampen even more. The hunger in his eyes matches my own, and the tent in his pants has me unabashedly pushing back into him.

With a groan, his hand grips my hip while his pincer arm bends around my waist as he leans his body over mine, grinding himself into me and cursing under his breath.

"Pool," Nanuk says suddenly in an almost bark, making us both jump.

Way to kill the mood again, bear.

"He can't teach you properly anyway because of his pincer," Nanuk says, continuing to fuck up Operation Seduction, and I scowl at him as Styng uses the distraction to slink away from me, adjusting his junk as he does.

I refuse to lose this battle and instead focus my attention on Tallon. "You're absolutely right. Tallon? Help a needy girl out?"

His eyes light up, and he steps toward me, even as Alfa tries and fails to grab him. *Good boy.* Without an ounce of hesitation, he rounds me and leans his body into mine, bending me over the table and directing my hands on the stick to the right places, and to my disappointment goes straight into tips on how to make a good shot. *You've got to be kidding me?*

With a sigh, I focus on what he's saying as best as I can while my body is burning from the inside out, and I look up to find Venom straight across from me, his focus completely lost down my low cut shirt, my breasts almost completely out on display from this angle.

I line up my pool cue and hit the white ball with a clang, making sure to press back into Tallon while catching Venom's attention, using my fingers to trail the curve of my right breast as I stand back up.

The room groans at my movement, and I smile at Venom. "How did I do?"

"Okay, is it just me, or is Faun trying to find a mate? Because between her hot as fuck smell and the way she keeps presenting herself, my dick is harder than Chuck Norris," Steve moans, cupping his cock through his pants to make his point.

Tallon lets go of me and steps back, saying with a resigned sigh, "He's right, precious, what's going on?"

I start to tremble all over as the burning continues to rise, even though the temperature in the room has begun to cool dramatically. "You don't understand," I complain and lift my now shaking fingers to my hot temple, sweat beginning to bead there. "I need help."

If the atmosphere was cooling before, it is damn near freezing now, as my pack's faces become stoic and hard at my declaration. No doubt, their protective natures are rearing to life.

"What's wrong?" Ironside growls, ready to fight whatever monster I'll throw his way. His gargantuan muscles bulge at the very idea that I'm in peril.

Nanuk steps closer, his eyes narrowed with concern. "Has it got something to do with you going to the doctor so much lately? Are you sick?"

I nod, looking down at the ground, trying to figure out how to say what's going on with me without losing every shred of dignity that I have left. My mind hazes over with another wave of heat and my core starts to pulse again, and my dignity can go fuck itself at this point.

"I'm in heat for the first time, and I'm not coping well. I can't handle it anymore. I'm burning up more and more every day, and it hurts. Morigan said that I need to find a partner to help me through it, or it will become almost unbearable." I look up at them, my eyes now wet with unshed tears as I plead, "Please help me. Anyone."

If I thought it was quiet before, it has nothing on how silent it is now. Every male in this room stops breathing, and my heart drops at the horror written all over their faces.

CHAPTER 7
ALFA

BLOODY HELL.

I'm an excruciating mix of terrified, shocked, and majorly turned on, and from the looks of it, I'm not the only one.

We all just stand there with wide eyes and mouths, staring at the stunning creature before us, pleading for one of us to take her. Not in a million years would I have ever expected this. Dreamt it, sure, more times than is healthy to admit, but pictured it in reality, no bloody way!

The palpable tension in the room is so thick that you could cut it with a knife, and I want to say something to fix it, but I'm literally speechless; all words I've ever learned are completely forgotten by my tongue.

A single tear streaks down Faun's flawless golden cheek, and both guilt and regret instantly floor me at how I reacted to her vulnerability. It would have been so hard for her to admit it to us so publicly, especially after the way she was offering herself up so openly beforehand.

I step forward and put my hands up, wanting to stop her tears, and she looks at me hopefully, but still, no words come, and all I can do is move my lips like a fish pathetically.

What can I do? I can't help her. My teeth and claws are too sharp, my beast too wild, and the way my dick knots when I cum could really hurt her for all I know.

Dropping my head in shame, unable to look at her pleading eyes anymore, I shake my head and step back, my gut-wrenching at rejecting her in a time of need.

"I see." Faun's voice breaks, and so does my heart.

"It's not you," Steve says, as a matter of fact, but she just laughs coldly. "It's not. Well, not really."

That sounds even worse. We all glare at him for once again being a total idiot.

Tallon groans out, "Please stop trying to help Steve. For all that is good in this world, do not say another word."

"It's Crush," he grumbles under his breath as he plonks himself on the couch with a huff.

I roll my eyes and shake my head at his childish antics. Turning to Faun again, I feel sick as I take in her body, trembling and turning in on itself. *We can't just leave her like that, can we?*

"Faun, precious, I'm so sorry," Tallon whispers, trying to put his arm around her shoulders, but she shoves it off and her accusatory gaze travels over all of us.

"Go fuck yourself. I thought we were a pack, but I'm just a stray that you felt bad for," Faun says shakily, more tears streaming quietly down her face. "At least now I know where I stand."

FAUN

I knew it was risky to put myself out there like that, but I wasn't prepared to be publicly humiliated by the people I trust most in the world. The way they all stared at me with pity in their eyes will stick with me forever.

"I think I'd better go," I mumble, defeated. "If not one of you can even stomach touching me like that, then there is no reason for me to be in here."

Turning, I storm out of the room, and I'm instantly annoyed to smell Steve and Tallon on my tail. Not my real tail, of course, my proverbial one. These guys don't even know I have an actual tail. It's small and fluffy and way too close to my ass to be flashing people.

I ignore their presence and continue my angry path all the way to my room, where I promptly slam the door on Tallon's shocked face, his owl eyes wider than normal at my move. If he hadn't stepped back just in time, it would have given his beak-like nose a serious trim.

"Faun." I hear him plead behind the heavy wood, but I turn the lock and dive on my bed, throwing my pillow over me and screaming into my mattress.

It's not like I expected them to all lineup and ask for a go, but I was hoping that at least one of them might see me as more than just prey. I deserve to be seen as a woman, too.

If I didn't know better, I would think that they see me as a little sister, but I have felt more than one hard dick against me lately. So what's the issue?

Their rejection has hurt me way more than I'd like to admit; and for the first time since my dear friends were taken from me all those years ago, I feel truly alone in this world.

I am, after all, Ark's biggest disappointment.

DEBATING on whether I want to go to breakfast, I sulk in bed as someone knocks hard on the bedroom door.

"Faun, you've been in here long enough," Mayne all but growls. "Dinner last night was one thing, but you're not missing another meal. Pull your big girl panties on and let's go."

I roll my eyes and snuggle in deeper. *Nope. Breakfast is a no-go.*

"Don't make me knock your door down because I will, and you

know it. Then you'll never have a moment of privacy. Is that what you want?" Mayne threatens.

With a huff, I throw my blankets off and head toward the door, my heat still traveling over my body, because at this point I'm not getting a moment of peace from it.

I unlock it and rip the door open. "I'm coming," I snap at Mayne. His hand paused in the air as if he was about to knock again.

I'm only dressed in some booty shorts and a loose white tank top with no bra on because I just got out of bed. But Mayne has pissed me off, so I push past him still wearing next to nothing, and storm toward the dining hall.

Styng catches up to me, with Mayne trailing behind. "I get wanting to piss him off, but are you sure you want to go into the dining hall dressed like that?" he says, worry lining his voice.

"Abso-fucking-lutely."

Pushing open the double doors, I head straight for the food, picking up a banana and two pieces of toast already buttered. The whole while, I can feel a myriad of eyes on me.

My heat flares up again because of the proximity of so many males, but I ignore it and move to the nearest empty table, plonking my ass down so hard that my tits bounce.

I devour my toast quickly, hungry from not eating anything in ages. My table slowly fills up with my so-called pack in the meantime, but I never once take my focus off my food, refusing to give any of them the time of day.

"Morning, precious," Tallon greets me, sliding into the seat to my left, and I grunt in a very unladylike way. "Ookaayy," he drawls.

"Don't bother," Mayne snaps from across the table. "She's in a mood this morning. Maybe she's getting her period."

My eyes snap up to his, and I glare at him, the full force of my anger and disappointment in him drilling into his head. "If you can recall, dickhead, I'm in heat and need relief. Unfortunately, there's no one man enough at this table to help me out," I reply, in an over-the-top loud voice, which in hindsight was not the best idea I've ever had.

One of the Broken hyena men stands up and grabs his junk lewdly. "I've got something that can help with that, doe."

My table erupts in a mixture of growls from my pack at his outburst, but his table just laughs in response as he sits back down with a smug grin on his face.

Then the guard closest to me walks over with a heavy gait and leans on the end of the table with a smirk. "What's wrong, venison? These animals not able to perform like they should? If you ever want a real cock to ride, just let me know, and I'll take one for the team." He winks at me and looks at each one of the angry faces surrounding me, daring them to say something.

Because fuck them, I say in response, "I might just do that."

"Faun," Sting warns under his breath, but I hold my head up high and give the guard my full attention. I can't remember his name, but I really don't care at this point, if it means finding a bit of relief from the hell I'm going through.

Unfortunately, as I'm always the gag of every joke, he just laughs and walks away, telling the other guards how desperate I am.

I feel Tallon's hand slide to my shoulder, but I flick it off. "Don't touch me," I snap. The burning is eating me alive, and my ass wriggles on the seat, desperate for relief.

Last night, I brought myself several orgasms trying to make the pain stop, but it just seemed to make it worse.

"Why aren't any of the other females going through this?" I snark irritably.

As usual, my timing and luck are impeccable, as a female Broken black bear passes behind me on her way to her table and answers, "Because men actually want to fuck us." Her laughter is boisterous at my expense and seems to set off the whole room.

Wanting to get up and run from the room, absolutely mortified at what's happening, I gather all of my bravery and look each one of my so-called-pack in the eyes before I reply. "Lucky you. I'm just a pet with no purpose. It's a real shame because I have a lot more to offer."

With that, I pick up my banana and slowly peel off the entire skin, discarding it on my plate, and then I bring the banana to my mouth, eyes on Mayne across from me as I stick it in my mouth and down my throat, swallowing it whole.

His eyes bug out of his head the entire time, and he holds his breath until I stand up and lean over toward him. "Your loss is someone else's gain," I remark, standing with a confident smile that I really don't feel on the inside, and I stare the room down.

"I may be prey in a world of predators, but I'm willing and ready if any males want to help ease me through my heat. You know where my room is," I announce loudly to the room before I turn and leave, unable to look back for fear of more outright rejection.

CHAPTER 8
TALLON

Since Faun's terrifying proposition in the dining hall two days ago, it's been constant chaos trying to keep every Tom, Dick, and Harry away from her room.

While we want her to feel some relief, we sure as heck aren't letting other males go anywhere near her if we can't. I personally don't think there's any risk to her safety from us, but I will follow the pact in order to not create a rift between our pack.

The biggest of us have been posted outside her door and at her side constantly, but I've been charged with observation duty. My incredible eyesight and hearing are a huge advantage to catching any possible threats early on, but never was I expecting to uncover this.

"Dr. Micheals," Antonio greets the head scientist responsible for our existence. "What are you doing out here today?"

I was going to keep moving on, but something made me decide to spare a moment to observe their interaction quietly, and lucky I did.

"Antonio, mate, how's things?" he replies in his thick Australian accent. "Just thought I'd pop in and see how my little fellas are doing."

The guard laughs heartily. "I don't know about little, but they're still holding strong and evolving. Some more than others. I still don't know why you bothered making the deer bitch. She's useless as fuck."

"True, but now that we know more about the successes and failures, I can make sure the next round is more specific to our needs. Obviously, we won't be wasting our time with any more Broken prey, and some predators were a bit of a waste of time as well," the schmuk of a scientist says, and I have to hold my outrage in at him. And what's with this 'next time' that he's blundering about?

"Speaking of, how much longer do we have to put up with this lot before we go to phase two?" Antonio asks, piquing my curiosity once again.

"Is it safe to talk here?" Dr. Micheals asks quietly, and Antonio must have given a non-verbal affirmation because he continues on. "Well, if they continue to grow and develop well over the next year and a half, we should be ready to move to phase two."

Antonio asks, "What's going to be the difference between this lot and the next ones?"

"Apart from the obvious things like not including the splicing of creatures that won't be useful to the government, we will put them into the rigorous process of training and specialized development from as early as they're able to walk. None of this free-range rubbish. Phase one was just to see if they could develop and grow well without any major health or mental setbacks. Luckily, there has been a sufficient growth of aggression and strength in the majority of cases, which is a good indication that phase two should be a stellar success. Of course, it will mean a more rigorous structure and schedule for you and the other staff, but you should, if everything works out well, have loyalty and submission once you've established dominance over them."

"How do we do that?"

"Well, we have a few programs that we've made up for you to test, so we will probably split phase two into three groups to see how they run separately, and then focus on the most successful application. Either way, it's not going to be a fun ride for the Broken."

Dr. Micheals laughs at himself and continues, an apprehensive feeling traveling down my spine in warning. "I'm not looking forward to the diaper stage again, but I am excited to see how soon we can get results from the programs we're creating."

I shake my head in disgust at how flippantly these humans talk about our existence. Yes, we were made in a laboratory, but we deserve the same rights and care as any human does. We didn't ask for this, and we're worth more than a number in a program. Where are they planning to keep them all? Will they be mixed in with us? Will they be adding us into this new preposterous system they're discussing?

Antonio laughs. "It's not exactly like you and I have to change them. Hopefully, we can get some of those hot nannies in. I could use a little servicing, if you know what I mean?"

The two of them share in their amusement, while I silently seethe in my hidden corner. Humans are disgusting creatures, creating new life, just to then treat it like dirt, never appreciating what a gift it is to be free and always wanting more than what they've got. Perhaps they would see things differently if they were the ones locked away, defined only by their image and not the merit of their souls.

Luckily it's me who is overhearing this ludicrousy and not one of my pack mates because there's no chance that they'd be able to listen to these men's total disregard for our right to live and not get themselves into trouble. Out of all of us, Styng and I are definitely the most level-headed of our pack.

"Hey Doc, did you hear about that deer bitch throwing herself at everyone in the dining hall? It was fucking hilarious. She has a whole group of Broken predators at her beck and call, but even they won't stuff her taco. How embarrassing is that?" Antonio tells him, wheezing with laughter. "She's not even half bad for a freak. Some of the others are just gross to look at, but she only has antlers as far as I can tell. Cut them off, and you wouldn't even know she was a Broken."

"Oh, she has a tail, too. You just can't see it with her clothes on, but I agree. As far as the Broken go, she's definitely the best looking of the lot. It's a damn shame. I'd almost fuck it if I was desperate enough," Dr. Micheal adds, both appalling me and shocking the hell out of me. *She has a tail?* How on earth was I not aware of that? "I've been surprised for years that they don't just have her locked somewhere to use her for sex. She's not really good for anything else, and now you're telling me that they won't even touch her like that? That's interesting. I'll have to add it to my notes when I get back."

"It's true," Antonio replies. "I wonder if it's because she's not freaky enough to look at for them, or if it's just because she's too weak for them to want to?"

"Have you seen her with any of the other doctors lately? Maybe someone has some notes I can copy."

Antonio proceeds to tell Dr. Micheals about how Faun has been in and out to see Dr. Morigan Adina several times over the last month, and he is way too interested in that information for my comfort.

"Is Morigan seeing someone?" Antonio asks the Doc.

"Yeah, nah. She's married to the job, that one. I've tried to get in her pants a few times, but she won't have a bar of me. I reckon she's a lesbian, but a good bit of dick will loosen her up a bit," Dr. Micheals says, and I want to punch him in the face. I'm not normally a violent man, but these two seem to bring it out of me.

It's males like them that give the rest of us a bad name. Who cares what her sexual preference is? It's none of their business, and if anything, their nasty ass cocks would probably turn her away from men for life.

Having had enough of their revolting discussion, I stand, getting ready to move away, when Antonio asks something that has me frozen in my departure.

"When are we extinguishing phase one again?"

"On their twenty-first year. We'll let them get to full adulthood first, just in case there are any latent issues, but then we're clear to terminate them," Dr. Micheals answers as if what he's saying is as easy as the weather forecast, and I feel sick to my stomach. "If you ask me, though, we've got all the data that we need at this point. We have a meeting in a couple of months to discuss the possibility of moving the date forward. So we'll see."

No fucking way. They can't be serious.

"It won't come soon enough, I suspect. I'm over this lot. It'll be good to start fresh with Broken that we can mold into the soldiers they'll be useful as." Antonio sounds just as bored as Dr. Micheals. "Maybe I should sample that prey girl before we gas them. See if I can make her bleat."

Oh, my God. They are *serious.*

The entire contents of my stomach threaten to escape as my world tumbles upside down. While I always knew I was an experiment, I never put a lot of thought into what they were going to do with us. I figured that one day they would just train us for something; and I was a little more concerned about where Faun would fit in the grand scheme of things, but never did I think that they'd just eliminate all of us and start again.

Immediately, I take off as quietly as I can to avoid any notice from the two monsters around the corner, and I don't stop until I run into Alfa. My face must show my growing fear because he instantly freezes what he's doing and meets me halfway.

"What's happened?" he asks without preamble.

I shake my head and tell him that we all need to talk, now, and without Faun.

Deciding to leave her with Sabre and Venom, the two of us gather the others in my room, and once they're all present, I have to take a deep breath and decide where to start.

CHAPTER 9
STYNG

I DON'T KNOW WHAT I EXPECTED TO COME OUT OF TALLON'S mouth. Maybe something else about how shit we've been making Faun feel, but never in a million years could I have prepared for what he said.

Sitting down on his bed, his head down in astonishment, he explains to us everything from the conversation he overheard between Antonio and Dr. Micheals, and I swear I throw up in my mouth a little.

"You're absolutely sure that's what you heard?" Mayne asks cautiously, and the death stare he receives in reply is enough to make it solidify. We're all going to die. Faun is going to die, and there's nothing we can do to save her.

The desperation I suddenly feel to get to her side and hold her tight is overwhelming, and it takes all my effort to stay put. I've wasted this long trying to keep her at arm's length for her own safety, just to have her killed anyway. It's more than I can stomach, and from the looks of the males around me, nobody is taking this news well.

"We need to get out of here," Ironside snaps, starting to pace back and forth, his muscles bulging like he's ready to just smash the walls in between him and freedom down.

After a few seconds of us all staring in silence, trying to come to terms with what's in store for us and how indispensable we really are, a knock sounds on the door, and I jump slightly. My hearing isn't as good as most of the others, so I didn't hear anyone approaching.

Steve opens it and Faun, Sabre, and Venom stroll in, looking around with confusion.

"Where do we need to get out of?" Faun asks the room, but no one answers her, because what can we say?

Moving over to her, I take her hand, even though she tries to pull it from me because she's still angry as fuck at us. Looking at Sabre with a knowing glance, I say, "I'm gonna hang out with Faun for a while. Why don't you guys hang out here with these smelly fucks? Nanuk, want to come with us?" I'm more than aware that I shouldn't be alone with her, even now.

When he moves over to me without a word, I turn and leave the room, pulling Faun along with me, her hand still trying to get free of mine; but I'm desperate to touch her right now and don't have the strength in me to let go.

Instead, I smile at her and ask, "Want to play Monopoly? I'll let you be the car."

Board games have always been her greatest weakness, and as if on cue, she stops trying to pull away from me and says, "What do you mean, 'let me'? I'm always the car, you know that." For prey, she has a wicked competitive streak.

Nanuk and I laugh, and as we walk, I think of an awesome joke that she'll love. "Hey, baby, what happens when a chicken, cow, and pig walk into a BBQ?"

"What?" she asks, perking up despite her understandable anger because Faun loves dad jokes.

I stop and stare at her until she raises her brows and say, "Nothing, obviously." It takes her a second, but then she bursts out laughing, covering her mouth with her spare hand, and Nanuk just shakes his hand at me, unimpressed, as usual. The only ones with a sense of humor around here apart from me are Faun and Steve, and to be fair, Steve's idea of a joke is way dirtier.

"That's terrible," Faun giggles.

I laugh at her. "But still you laugh. You know you're going to hell, right?"

She slaps my chest. "Hey, that's no fair. You told the joke, you should go to hell, not me."

"I never said you were going alone." I grin down at her, but my humor dies as I remember how close we actually are to death, so I freeze my smile on my face, not wanting to worry her. I catch Nanuk's gaze and can tell straight away that his mind went to the same place mine did, and I hope my eyes are hiding my sadness better than his.

"Okay, give me another one, but not one I'll feel bad about," Faun demands, smiling now as we walk toward the common room nearest us.

I've got hundreds of them and am always happy to make her smile. "Which bear is the most condescending?" I ask, eyeing the Broken polar bear beside us with a grin.

"You'd better watch it," he grumbles, but I know he doesn't mean it.

"A pan-duh," I answer with an exaggerated, "bad-dum-cha."

"Oh. My. God. Just kill me," Nanuk says with a sigh, while Faun and I laugh at its ridiculousness.

Faun cries, "More," but Nanuk growls under his breath. She pokes her tongue out at him and asks, "Come on, just one? I know who's the grumpy bear."

Nanuk throws his head back with a, "Fine, one more."

Happy that she won, she smiles at me expectantly, and her perfect face takes my breath away. The way her eyes light up when she's happy feels like the sun kissing your skin on a freezing cold day: warm, welcome, and like home.

"Why did the fish blush?" I ask after I clear my throat, trying to concentrate and not get lost in her eyes. She wrinkles her nose as she waits for my answer. "Because it saw the ocean's bottom."

Choking on her own spit, Faun splutters and laughs at the same time. Her face goes bright red, and she bends over, trying to catch her breath.

"Something is seriously wrong with you two," Nanuk groans, as he picks up the Monopoly from the shelf and starts to lay it all out on the table in the middle of the room.

I pat her on the back and rub my hand in circles. "You alright there?" I ask, while laughing. When she settles down, I pick her up, carry her over to the table, and plonk down on the carpet, placing her comfortably in my lap, as I'm used to doing. Forgetting for a second that we've been keeping more of a distance from her at the moment.

"I'm better now," she answers, snuggling in with a contented sigh, and I don't have the heart to move her. Nor do I want to. She must have seen something on Nanuk's face because she asks him, "What were you guys talking about earlier that was so important I needed to be squirreled away?"

"Please don't ask me, pretty girl. All I ever do is make stuff sound worse, and I'm not sure what I'm not supposed to tell you," Nanuk answers blandly.

Really? He couldn't just say 'nothing'. "It was just guy stuff, nothing for you to worry about, baby," I add, hoping that it'll help but doubt it.

Thankfully, she lets it go with a disapproving huff, and we all get into the game, but I find my concentration constantly ripped away, our fate riding me hard.

We've always talked about getting out of here someday, somehow, but in the past, that has always seemed like a long-lost dream; something that sounds lovely, but no one really believes is going to happen. Everything is different now. It's not a dream anymore. Now it's a desperate plea for survival because if we don't find a way to escape this place, then we're all doomed.

Somehow, I need to work out how to turn that dream into a

reality. If not for me and our pack, then at least for Faun. She deserves to live. We all do.

FAUN

I know they're keeping something big from me, but if I've learned anything since joining their pack, it's that they won't tell me shit if they don't want to.

Looking over at Nanuk, I try to figure out the best strategy to pick his brain for information, because he has a constant foot in mouth syndrome and is terrible at keeping secrets.

"Don't even think about it," Styng whispers in my ear, giving me goosebumps all over my skin, my heat picking up a notch.

I watch in fascination as Nanuk's nose twitches and his eyes pop up to mine, hungry and frustrated. "I don't know what you're talking about. I'm just sitting here minding my own business, kicking your butts, and taking all your money," I say innocently, batting my eyelashes as I look at him over my shoulder.

"Uh, huh. You weren't at all trying to come up with a scheme to pump us for information," Styng adds sarcastically.

"Exactly. See, innocent."

Nanuk scoffs and lands on my Park Place. "Ha! Pay up sucker!" I yell, bouncing up and down. "Who's your mama now?"

"Careful, there's valuable merchandise under there. I don't need you smashing my family jewels with your evil excitement," Styng complains, and I move to sit beside him with an apology, but can't stifle a laugh as he cups himself with a pained expression.

"Now, that's funny," Nanuk snorts, and Styng flips him the bird.

I go to roll the dice but stop, looking at both of them. "Seriously though, you guys have had your fun, and I played along, but I have the feeling that I have a right to know what you lot were talking about." Silence answers me, and neither of them looks in my direction, telling me that I'm not going to like it at all. "Is it about me?" Still nothing. "I swear to God, if you guys just had a meeting to talk about how pathetic and desperate you think I am now, I'm going to pay Ironside with a year's worth of pudding to pee in all your shoes."

They both wrinkle up their faces because they know he'll do it for an extra serving of pudding for the whole year.

I grab Styng's pincer to get his full attention and try one more time, hoping that he respects me enough to at least be honest with me. "What's going on?"

I see a flutter of guilt in his eyes before he smiles and says jokingly, "We were organizing a flash dance to surprise you, but now you're gonna have to miss out. Such a shame because Sabre and Mayne were going to wear silver hot pants and nothing else. Would've been epic."

"If only you hadn't been nosey. Oh, well," Nanuk adds, going along with Styng's bullshit.

I give them a small, flat smile, unable to muster anything else, and say, "Pity." I roll the dice and deflate even more inside.

CHAPTER 10
IRONSIDE

As I wait for Dr. Foster Adina, I can't help but pray that he and his daughter are as good as they have appeared over the years. While they've only ever shown us kindness and understanding, they're still employees of the Ark at the end of the day. So, it gives me a realistic amount of anxiety sitting here, about to confide in him behind everyone's back.

However, I have enough confidence in my intuition that I came here regardless, willing to risk any consequences that could come my way, especially if it means helping Faun and the others survive.

I'm not even sure that he'll see me, because he's not as easy to get an appointment with as Dr. Morigan Adina, who is very much our main medical caregiver.

My suspicions are confirmed when the random guard on duty takes me to the daughter's office instead. Not that I mind, because I'm sure she can tell him what we're about to talk about.

Thankfully, Antonio is nowhere to be seen today. That guy hangs around her room like a bad smell, and the last thing I need today is his fuck face hovering.

After the guard knocks, Dr. Adina opens the door with a bored look on her face until she sees me standing behind him, and her eyes light up as she greets me.

"Hey, Doc," I say, smiling back, and she closes us in the room, sitting in her usual spot. With long, easy strides, I join her, squeezing into the admittedly too small armchair. That's not her fault though. For anyone else it's a decent size, but I am the biggest person I've seen to date, and I'm not so sure they make chairs in my size. "How's business? We all keeping you on your toes?"

With a light laugh, she replies, "As usual."

"No one's giving you any trouble, are they?" I ask, concerned. "Let me know, and I'll have a talk to them."

"No. No. Nothing like that, but I appreciate the sentiment. You've always been one of the good guys. And I'm not just talking about in here. You and your pack trump most human men by a mile in the manners department," Doc says with a shake of her head. "Now, how can I help today? Is this about Faun?"

I shift in my seat, looking away guiltily at that. Now that we all know what she needs, we've been avoiding her as much as we can, but we already know where Doc stands on that front. "Ah, no."

Doc looks at me with a knowing look over the top of her glasses. "Mmm-hmm." I can feel her judgment like a thick haze, and I feel obligated to defend myself.

"We can't, okay? It's not like none of us want to. It's just that she's not like us, and if in the heat of the moment we crushed her or poisoned her or bit and clawed her, we would never forgive ourselves. We made a promise a long time ago that we were going to protect her, and we're not about to stop now just because we want to get in her pants."

"Have you ever taken into consideration how much pain she's in right now because you're *protecting* her?" Doc asks me. "While you're trying to be chivalrous, Faun is in constant agony that could be easily rectified by just one of you. I have no doubt that she understands the risk, but it must be very hurtful and confusing for her."

Not wanting to think about what she's saying to me, because I'm already feeling guilty enough at the moment without her ramming it home, I get to the point. "I don't mean to be offensive, but like I said, I'm not here to talk about Faun. Tallon overheard Antonio and Dr. Micheals talking about something very disturbing, and I wanted to know if it's safe for me to talk to you about it?"

Her frown deepens in thought. "I don't know what it could be that you would need to talk to me about it."

"It's about us being phase one," I say cryptically, but her eyes instantly widen, and she sits forward in keen interest, her elbows leaning on her knees.

"What did you hear?" Doc quickly asks.

Deciding that I've come this far, I might as well just go for it, I say, "Dr. Micheals told Antonio that he was getting ready for phase two since we were mostly a success."

"You were never kept in the dark about being experiments. So, why are you surprised that they would want to continue their studies?" she asks me curiously.

"That's not what has us on edge, even though I still think it's pretty fucked up. It's more the extermination of phase one that I have an issue with."

Doc sucks in a deep breath and sits straight up. "What are you talking about? What extermination?"

I'm on the fence on whether to believe her show of innocence, but her reaction seems quite sudden and unexpected.

"The one we are meant to have at twenty-one. Are you seriously going to sit there and pretend that you don't know anything about it?" I ask, needing her to be honest with me.

Her eyes shift away guiltily and my stomach drops. *She does know.* "I guess I know the answer to that question, then," I mumble, slouching in the chair in defeat, or at least as much as I can at my size.

Doc exhales in a puff and says quietly, "I need you to listen very carefully, Ironside. While I do know about the initial plan to eliminate phase one before starting phase two, I know my father is working very hard to rectify that behind the scenes, and we're very hopeful about the outcome."

"That's not what Tallon heard," I throw back, grumpily. "Seems the good Dr. Micheals has meetings coming up revolving around canceling phase one early, because we're not of any use to him anymore, in his opinion. He seemed *very* confident about this new timeline."

"No. That can't be right. We would have been told," Dr. Adina says as she gets up and starts pacing the room, highly agitated. "Give me a minute."

Rushing behind her desk, she picks up her phone and dials a number, before waiting patiently until the other person answers. "Dad, did you hear about Dr. Micheals bringing forward the extermination of the Broken?" she asks, getting right to the point.

I watch her face as Dr. Foster Adina talks through the line, and I am starting to believe what she's saying to me as her eyes become wet and her features get visibly upset.

They talk together as she explains what I found out to him. "We need to do something." She waits. "I know, but we need to do it faster. I have Ironside here with me." Her eyes flick toward me. "Yes. No problem."

Doc's hand reaches out with the phone for me to take, and I stand up, taking the device from her, looking at it with wonder. I've seen them plenty of times but have never held one before. Cautiously, I bring it to my ear and say, "Hello?"

"Ironside, we have no time to waste. Did you hear exactly when Dr. Micheals thought that this might be happening? Any information that you might know could be very useful if I'm going to be able to help," the father half of the duo says in a rushed tone.

"Tallon said something about a couple of months," I tell him, happy that he's taking this seriously. "Why do you both want to help us? We're just experiments to you," I ask him while looking at his daughter in question.

Dr. Morigan Adina shakes her head, looking sad, but her dad

answers me. "You are so much more than that, and don't you forget it. The moment you were all born, I made a promise that I would look out for you and protect you the best I can because you deserve to live just as much as we do."

"Thank you, sir." My voice breaks at the end, touched that these people actually give a damn about us at all.

"You're welcome, son. Put my daughter on for me, please, and take care of yourself. If I were you, though, I'd keep that information to your pack for now, in case the more aggressive Broken find out and riot. If something like that happens, all it will do is strengthen Dr. Micheals' case."

Agreeing, I pass the phone over and tune out the rest of their conversation, my mind wondering about our fate and what we can do to help our own survival.

Doc hangs up and tells me, "I can only say so much to you about this, but I can say that there are people in the background who believe just as vehemently as we do that you all deserve the right to survive and thrive. They have been doing what they can on the sidelines, but in the meantime, my father and I have been working on our own potential back-up plan in case something like this happened. You need to keep this on the down-low as well, because if I'm being completely frank with you, not all the Broken are like your pack. There are some very savage people in here that would only be a threat to the human race, and while we want to help you, we can't, with a clear conscience, let our vicious killers into the world. If my dad and I continue with this possible escape plan, it will be only for the ten of you. Do you understand?"

The gravity of what she's saying to me sits heavily on my chest, but if I'm being honest with myself, she's absolutely right. People like Syla and Adda would find pleasure in killing and destroying the weakest prey they could find, which would be children, and I don't want that on my conscience, either.

"How can you be so sure that we won't be a risk to humans?" I ask, genuinely curious and a little nervous because I would hate to be the reason someone got hurt.

Doc smiles at me with total confidence and says, "Because of how you are with Faun and with me. I have never seen any aggression from any of you that wasn't a direct reaction to protecting those who can't protect themselves. That being said, you won't be able to mingle with humans if we manage to get you out. It's important that you remember that. Otherwise, you could end up in a place much worse than this, and you don't want that. Trust me."

I nod in acknowledgment and am endlessly glad that I decided to come in here today, because if I hadn't said anything, then they wouldn't have known. I don't know if they'll be able to save us from the fate mapped out by Dr. Micheals, but at least I know there's someone on our side trying.

CHAPTER 11
STEVE

I don't see what the big deal is? Why the hell are we keeping all of this from Faun? It doesn't seem right to me because she has a right to know what's going on.

Sitting next to Alfa on the couch, I gaze over at Faun longingly as she sulks on the other side of the room in front of the TV, watching some girly crap about glittery vampires.

I roll my eyes, irritated because Faun has been pretending that we aren't here, and it's getting old. I asked Venom about it earlier, and he said she was pissed off with us because every one of us has been refusing her sexually.

Stuff that crap. As soon as I get any kind of go-ahead from the others, I'm going to be balls deep in that woman before she can blink. My wrist is getting sore as hell over jerking off and fantasizing about her every second of the day that I'm not with her.

Fucking cock blockers.

I picture her bent over the arm of the chair she's sitting in as I watch my hard cock glide in and out of her wet cunt, her mouth full of Alfa, choking on him as he fucks her face.

My body visibly shudders, and Alfa turns to look at me with a raised eyebrow. No doubt he can smell my want for the woman before us, but I just wink, unashamed, and push myself off the chair.

With my gaze now a laser focus on the object of my desire, I stalk toward her, intent on getting her to touch me in some way, any way, at this point.

I sit in front of her on the floor, taking her hand in mine as I sit back on my heels. "I'm always here for you, you know? I might come across as the crazy one of the group, but I have a heart too. If you need anything, all you have to do is ask," I tell her, letting my softer side shine through. I want her to see me as I am on the inside, and not just the jokester.

The truth is that I *will* always be there for her. Whether we only have a couple of months left or a long life ahead of us, I won't ever let her go, and I'll never let anything happen to her if I can help it. Even if it means I can never have her in the way I want... And I do want it, I want it badly. I want her smile, her tears, her vulnerability, and her strength. I want her brilliant mind, her beautiful heart, and her luscious body, and I don't mind sharing her if it means that she's also mine. Now all I have to do is convince eight stubborn males that she's safe with us because I truly believe she is. I know in my deepest heart that even when my beast is at his most ferocious, I would never hurt her.

After all, what is a beast without his heart?

"Do you mean that?" she asks me, stunning me out of my thought process.

Looking up at her bewitching face, I smile and answer, "Of course, forever."

Faun's eyes twinkle with mischief, and I watch with intrigue as her mind ticks over into something cheeky—instantly I know that shit's about to hit the fan.

I have a feeling I'm going to wish I'd stayed with Alfa.

FAUN

"Anything?" I ask, my interest piqued.

Trusty Steve. Always ready to give a needy girl a hand, and it just so happens that I have an itch that desperately needs to be scratched.

If anyone in my pack is going to help me out, it has got to be Steve, with his constantly dirty jokes, outright flirting with me, and his inhibition. My pussy burns at the thought of him between my legs, and I squirm in my seat, searching for some relief.

My scent must have just hit him because his nostrils open with an inhale, and Steve's eyes become hooded. Using the moment to my benefit, I open my legs up further and slide closer to him, his body now between my thighs, and I snuggle my face into his chest, careful not to hit him with my antlers. His big size is an advantage because even on his knees, he towers over me. I wrap my arms around him and look up at his big crocodile eyes; the light shining off them in an almost eerie way.

I bat my eyelashes at him innocently. "You are so good at being there for me. I never have to feel fear or anxiety when you're around because I know you'll protect me," I say, littering him with compliments that I mean. "You mean so much to me. Thank you for being here for me and saying that you'll help me."

Steve's big hands rub up and down my back, and he surprises me by kissing my forehead softly. "It's my pleasure."

"It could be," I answer suggestively, making him growl low in his throat.

Alfa suddenly growls low with warning from his side of the room, which is very unlike him, but it's obviously a reminder not to touch me. I ignore him, however, and focus my full attention on Steve.

With a quick move that I wasn't expecting, Steve puts his hands under my thighs and lifts me effortlessly into his arms as he gets up and turns around. He sits back down on the chair, but with me on his lap, straddling him.

His eyes hood with lust as I use my position to rub my swollen, aching pussy against the growing bulge in his pants. My head falls back, and an embarrassingly loud moan escapes my lips at the friction that I'm so desperate for, and I roll my hips again, this time harder.

"Fuck," Steve rumbles as his big hands grip my ass tightly, encouraging me to keep going.

Back and forth, I start to roll my hips in a steady motion as he guides me with his strong grip. My pussy is wet and pulsing with desire, the heat inside me roiling and bubbling with need.

"More. Don't stop," I cry out, unable to hold it in.

Our breaths start to mingle with my lips centimeters from his, and he groans, leaning forward to taste me, but I'm suddenly yanked from his lap. Alfa's hands holding me under my arms, but away from his body.

Alfa practically runs to the other side of the room, placing me down like I'm on fire, and retreats back to Steve in record time. He slaps Steve's dazed face hard, as if to break him from a stupor, and growls, "Are you bloody stupid?"

Steve ignores him, his eyes drilling a hole into me as he grips the huge, wet bulge in his pants. His steadfast gaze is longing and desperate. No doubt mirroring my own.

"What the fuck, Alfa! I'm hurting," I practically scream at him.

Steve tries to stand, clearly heading toward me, but Alfa pushes him down with a, "Stay there for everyone's sake."

I stride over, eyes locked on Steve. If he's willing to ignore Alfa's wishes, then so am I. I'm riding that hard dick today if it's the last thing I do. My pussy clenches in need and another moan escapes me as I near.

Alfa steps in between us, his normally soft eyes strangely wild, and I sneer between my teeth, "Get out of my way."

CHAPTER 12
ALFA

I CAN'T BLOODY DO THIS ANYMORE.

Faun's face is a perfectly flushed pink. Her lips are parted slightly, and her eyes heavy with lust as she stares past me at Steve. *That lucky bastard.* My eyes drop to her heaving breasts, and I inhale another large breath of her alluring scent.

I turn, looking down at Steve, needing to hide my growing erection from her, and find Steve in a no better state. I flick my gaze to his lap and have to stifle a groan at the wetness pooling there from Faun grinding against him. What I would give to taste her there.

"Stop being so desperate," I growl at her over my shoulder. I hate the words as they leave my mouth, but I have to do something to move her away, or Steve and I are both going to take her before we can get a hold of ourselves. My own control is barely there at the moment.

The other males in our pack choose that moment to walk in, stopping immediately and taking in the heavy scent of arousal in the air, my pained expression that she can't see from behind me, and Steve's hands digging hard into the chair below him, his eyes drinking her in.

My heart cracks when I hear a sob rip from Faun, and she cries out, "I don't understand. I need you, all of you, but none of you will help me. I can smell that you want me, but you won't freaking touch me."

Her little hands shove at my back. and I turn to see her cheeks already wet from my hurtful words—I want to rip them back into my mouth. Nothing is worth watching my Faun cry.

"Am I that hideous to you? Or is it because I'm weak? Or small?" She sobs, "Why can't you at least try, for me? I would do anything for you. I need you."

Her pleading damn near kills me. and Faun starts to sob hard, burying her delicate features in her dainty little hands, her shoulders shaking violently. Faun's softness and fragility have never been more obvious.

If only she knew that every single one of us has been head over heels for this angelic creature since the moment she came tumbling into our circle. The day she became ours to protect was the same day that she stole our hearts.

Somehow, we knew that day that she was always meant to be ours; Tallon knew even longer. The fact that she is loved so much by all of us is exactly why we can't touch her, can't let her seduce us. She is everything, and we will do everything we can to protect her at all costs.

FAUN

I stifle the next sob that desperately tries to escape me, wanting to gather whatever pride I have left.

Steve suddenly says, "I need you too." The room goes quiet as Steve turns to look at me with hopeful eyes, the others with accusatory ones. "What? Fuck you, bros! I'm not going to hurt her, and if you think you're going to, then that's a *you* problem, because I'm sick and tired of denying what I want, and what I want—and need—is Faun."

I look around the room, and everyone that means so much to me is glaring daggers at Steve, but he just smiles at me, and I can't help but smile back, releasing some weight off my shoulders knowing that I'm not alone in this anymore. I can see it in his eyes that he means what he just said, and that he's done staying away from me.

I don't know why everyone is so mad at him for telling me that, and I don't even care because I finally don't feel alone. This heat has been way harder on me than I've let on; the pain, the emptiness, the need, it's all just too much to bear, and I finally feel like I don't have to bear it on my own.

The smile on my face grows into a wide grin of joy, and I hold my arms out to Steve as I walk toward him, asking him silently if he'll meet me halfway. To my absolute delight, he does, stalking me like the predator he is. The difference now is that when he looks at me, he's seeing me like I'm no longer his prey, but an equal instead.

"Steve?" Sabre says to him. His voice comes out uncomfortable and nervous, but Steve ignores him, wrapping his arms around my waist and pulling me close to his body.

"Thank you," I say with all of my heart in my eyes. "Thank you so much. You won't be disappointed, I promise. I'll do the best I can."

Steve's finger closes over my lips, and he shushes me. "Don't say things like that, that's ridiculous. There's nothing you can do to disappoint me because there's nothing about you that's a disappointment. You're the light of my life, and I'm yours if you want me."

My arm is suddenly grabbed by Mayne, and he pulls me from Steve's embrace.

Steve growls in between his sharpened teeth at him, but Mayne steps between us, looking hard down at me, saying simply, "No."

"No," I say, "What do you mean no? You can't say no. This has nothing to do with you."

"It has everything to do with me," he growls and Steve tries to push around him, but Sabre gets involved and pushes him back.

"How has it got anything to do with you?" I ask Mayne, frustrated and angry that he's ruining this for me. "Why would it?"

"You don't understand! From the start, we've done everything we can to protect you. I'm not going to just stop caring and let you do this to yourself." I don't understand why Mayne is saying that, because it doesn't make any sense to me. I'm not doing anything dangerous, just succumbing to my needs, finally. All I want is relief.

I glare at him with all the menace that I can possess and ask, "You give me one good reason why this has anything to do with you? Or get the hell out of my way and out of my life."

The shock of my words has Mayne stepping back, his eyes wide as he looks down at me with horror. "That's right buddy, if you're going to continue making my life hard, then I don't want you in it. Even if that means breaking my own heart."

"It's a pact," Steve says from behind Mayne and Sabre.

"Steve," Sabre growls at him. "Don't."

"She's right. This has nothing to do with you guys. I've made my choice, and I have no doubt in my mind that I'm not going to hurt her, and I'm not gonna let you stand in the way and keep hurting her by denying her this," Steve says, defending me.

"What pact?" I ask, not letting it go.

I watch as Mayne's gaze looks away guiltily. But as he glances back at me, it's obvious that he can see the determination lining my gaze, because we both know that I'm stubborn as hell; and there's no way he's leaving this room without telling me what pact they're talking about.

He huffs out in exasperation, knowing that it's time to tell me everything. "When you came into our lives, you weren't expected; we were a pack of predators, and we really didn't associate with any kind of prey. Maybe it was some kind of discrimination. I don't know; we were young, and we never really thought about it, to be honest; but then you came rolling into our lives like a boulder, destroying everything we thought we knew. I'm not sorry about that, though. Don't get me wrong, it changed our lives, but in a way that made it better every single day. Tallon was right. He was always right. He knew that you would be a valuable asset to us, way before the rest of us did. I'm sorry that you lost your friends that day, beautiful, but I'm not sorry that you became a part of our pack."

"We value you, not just as a member of our pack, but also as a woman. You are gorgeous, smart, kind, thoughtful, and perfect in every single way. The strength you have inside you is a strength we'll never have because it's built from your beautiful soul. But the problem is—and it always will be—that you're physically too weak."

Some of the guys gasp, thinking that I'm about to snap from being called weak, but I know what he says is true, and denying it won't change the fact. What I am absolutely shocked about is the kind words that are coming out of his mouth. I don't understand what's going on exactly, but I've never heard him talk to me like this before. Mayne is generally stoic and grumpy. Yes, he's always had my back, but he's not exactly the type of guy who shows feelings. Stunned, all I can do is stand there quietly and listen because I have no words.

"We may have been young when you came into our lives, but we were males, nonetheless, and you are absolutely stunning. I don't think you realize the sexual prowess you actually have, or that you've been leading us by our dicks since the moment you became a part of our lives. From very early on, we had to have a meeting and talk about it, because it's clear that our strength and yours are two totally different things, and we needed to discuss it."

"We made a pact on that day that none of us would ever touch you like that, not because we didn't want you, but because you're not safe with us. We'll do everything we can to protect you, even if it means from ourselves, because inside us are very dangerous predators. We have poison, claws, sharp teeth, and incredible strength. What would happen to you if, in the heat of the moment, our beasts took over? You could really be hurt or killed, and we don't want to do that to you. We won't! You can need us as much as you want, but we won't falter our beliefs, because you're worth fighting to keep safe. You don't always have to like us, beautiful, but we will always love you; and if that means that you spend however much time we have left together grumpy because we won't give in, then so be it, because it's our job as your pack to take care of you. Do you understand?"

Mayne turns around and locks eyes with Steve. "I don't know how you managed to forget that, but you need to remember fast because if you love her the way you say you do, you won't do this."

I stare at his back in shock. There are a lot of things that he could have said to me today, but I never expected this. I think it's a stupid reason to stay away from me, even if I can grudgingly understand the thought process because I trust them and know they would never hurt me. Why can't they believe that too?

I look deep into each of the males' eyes surrounding me, and I see a mixture of hunger and fear there. The realization thrills me and only makes me more determined, whether they like it or not.

"Do you want me?" I ask the room, needing a last vestige of reassurance.

Mayne says nothing. He just stands there and stares at me, refusing to encourage my affections any further.

Behind him, Steve steps around, Sabre letting him. "We all do, and unlike these other cowards, I'm not afraid to tell you that. We always have, and we always will." He walks the rest of the way around to stand before me, and then taps me on the shoulder, randomly stating, "Shotgun." As always, he brings humor to a humorless situation.

Styng and Ironside can't help but laugh. Mayne, however, turns his trademark glare at them, trying to reign in the seriousness of the situation.

Steve's right! They do want me, and it's been right in front of me this whole time, but I was too stupid to see it. However, I see it now, and I'm never going to be able to unsee it again.

I come up with all the mental strength and determination that I know I'm going to need because I'm going to fight for them.

Not only that, but I *will* win, and they *will* be mine.

CHAPTER 13
VENOM

THE LAST TWO WEEKS HAVE BEEN THE ABSOLUTE WORST. Between Faun rubbing all over us deliberately whenever she can, and constantly walking around half-dressed, her pheromones have been boiling through the roof and tempting even our very best restraints.

I feel my control slip even further as I stand outside the shower door, blocking it from anyone else entering while Faun washes, her soft, humming voice carrying over the sound of cascading water. Steve was given duty outside the bathroom because we all agreed that he can't be trusted to be alone with her in here.

The thick steam from her hot shower mists the mirrors in the women's bathroom and I shift uncomfortably, adjusting my hard cock through my pants. My mind drifts to the thought of those searing droplets laving at her body, traveling down in thick rivulets over her taut nipples and down to her exposed pussy.

Licking my lips, I physically shake my head, trying to focus on anything else. *Antonio's hairy ball sack. Ironside's giant shit! Tallon's missing wings.* The last thought does it, sucking every bit of happiness at the memory of my brother sobbing quietly into his pillow while the fresh bandages on his back seep with a deep red as his vicious wound continues to bleed.

The water suddenly cuts off, pulling me from my morbid reverie and back to my current predicament. But at least now, I don't have a raging hard-on.

"Venom?" Faun's soft, husky voice calls out from behind the wooden shower door, her seductive tone instantly putting me on edge.

I clear my throat and ask cautiously, "Yeah?"

"I left my towel on the vanity out there. Can you please pass it to me?" she asks in the same voice, and I freeze, my eyes flicking to the white towel folded next to the sink.

Shit. She did that on purpose.

I stalk over and grab it, turning to her door and lifting the towel above my head to pass it over the top of the door, when it pulls open before I get a chance to. A thick roll of steam pours over me, licking up the sides of Faun's very wet, very naked body as it tries to escape the small confines, and I suck in a stunned breath.

Other than swallowing hard, my mouth as dry as dirt, the rest of my body seems frozen in position; the curves of her long, lithe body sucking out every brain cell I have, leaving me a fumbling mess, blood pooling to my cock.

Faun looks up at me temptingly, her eyes half-lidded and pleading for me to touch her. My gaze flicks down her body, traversing a slow path I've never had the privilege to travel. I never knew hands could get jealous of eyes until this very second.

The towel drops from my hands, landing unceremoniously on the floor as she steps toward me. My hands clench into tight fists as I fight every temptation to touch her glistening skin.

"You dropped my towel," Faun pants out, her breaths coming faster, making her breasts rise and fall, capturing my full focus.

Barely aware of what I'm doing, I slowly lower to my knees. My eyes still drilled into her light brown nipples that pop out like tight little chocolate balls, begging for me to taste them.

My hands fumble around carelessly for the lost fabric, as her mouth-watering aroma wafts around me, making me feel heavy with its ferocity, and I realize just how close I am to the source of the scent.

I watch in fascination as Faun's hands lift to the nipples that have captured me, pinching them slightly, and I suck in a breath, my dick painfully jumping in my pants.

In the back of my mind, I know I'm supposed to be remembering something important, but I can't quite grasp it.

One of Faun's hands leaves her succulent breast and slowly travels down her golden skin, and like a magnet, I can't look away. It travels lower and lower until her long, soft fingers brush through the soft apex of trimmed hair, her legs parting and her middle finger sliding through, doubling her already mouth-watering scent.

I growl deeply, my ass dropping to the heels of my feet in worship for the captivating creature before me, the towel all but forgotten.

Faun's breath hitches. I watch her finger dip inside her pussy, and the wet sound it makes, telling me how ready she is for me already, has me grabbing my dick hard through my pants with a pained groan.

Cursing under my breath, I feel as though all the air in my lungs has been ripped from me, and I am drowning in the desire to taste the juices I see dripping from her core as she starts slowly thrusting her finger inside her pussy again and again.

Her melodic moans reverberate off the white tiles throughout the bathroom, giving me an auditory delight that I have no doubt I'll cum over more than once in the dark recess of my room late at night.

"Don't stop," I tell her, unable to help it, my voice so husky that I barely recognize it. "I want you to cum for me. Show me what you like." I know this is wrong, but I can't find it in me to care.

Without delay, Faun's other hand drops to her core, swiping some of her juices up before rubbing rhythmic circles around her small swollen nub, eliciting a cry of pleasure from her parted lips.

I take her in from head to toe, my position on the floor almost perfect. Grabbing her calf, I whisper, "Trust me," and pull myself even closer, lifting her left foot and placing it on my thigh, opening her up to my feasting eyes even more.

She lets me without any complaint, and opens her knees even more, revealing her pussy completely to me, and I lick my lips like a man starved as she slides two fingers back inside her tight, moist hole.

Placing my hand over her other one, I guide it back to her clit, encouraging her to keep going, and she does it straight away. Wet noises fill the room, and I'm completely absorbed in what she's doing, needing to know how she likes to be touched and fantasizing that it's my fingers deep inside her, thrusting and getting soaked.

Faun's breathing hitches faster and her legs start to tremble as her tempo picks up. "That's it, Faun. Show me," I pant out, my own breathing so hard that I can barely catch it. "Cum for me."

With a wail of ecstasy, she lets loose, trembling with pleasure. Her core clenching like a vice over her fingers, and it takes every single ounce of strength not to close the distance to tasting her orgasm on my starving tongue.

Instead, I let her ride it out, stamping every movement to memory so that I can use this memory again, needing to cry out her name as I cum later tonight.

Her body starts to relax again, and I look up at her with reverence and unshielded lust, letting her see how much she affected me. Without losing eye contact, I reach forward, leisurely pulling her drenched fingers out of her and bringing them to my mouth.

With deliberate, slow movements, I bring one finger at a time to my open lips, sucking and licking them clean. I feel the vibrations through her fingers as she shivers in delight. Her sweet, almost butterscotch taste fills my taste buds. I never knew anything could taste so good, and I devour every drop of it. The intimacy of it, while locked in each other's gaze, makes my heart pound almost as hard as my cock.

A banging on the door makes us both jump; neither of our senses was paying attention to our surroundings, which is just another reason that I shouldn't have let this happen.

I drop her hand like it's the poisonous thing between us—not the teeth inside my mouth that I just had her vulnerable fingers in. *What the hell was I thinking?*

"Bro, are you guys coming? It's been freaking ages," Steve grumbles through the door, no doubt still sulking that I wouldn't let him be the one in here.

"We're coming. She's just drying herself now," I answer back as I pick up her towel, leaning past her naked body and placing it on the towel rack inside the shower cubicle. I whisper quietly to her, "You'd better quickly wash *that* off you." I point to her core but then turn around, walking back to the door, refusing to face her.

At first, I don't hear her move, but then she asks me with a disbelieving tone, "Are you serious? That's it? I could have done that without your assistance, but it's not enough."

I don't answer her or look over my shoulder, not wanting to face her disappointment.

"Look in my eyes and tell me you don't want me, you coward," she snaps at me, and I decide then and there to be completely honest.

Spinning on my heels, I stride back to her with fast movements, leaning into her bare skin and letting myself feel her close to me as I grab her hair tightly. I lift her face up to mine, and she whimpers in my hold, her hands flat on my chest, her hips grinding against my still hard cock unabashedly.

"I want to stick my dick so deep inside you and fuck you so hard that you see stars and feel me there for a week," I growl, lowering my lips to her, but not allowing them to touch. "I want to bury my face in between those tight thighs of yours, just so you can cum all over my face, and I can slurp up all of your butterscotch again and again." I pull her hair harder until she moans, and I breathe into her parted mouth, "I want you to slide my big black dick in between these hot lips, and then have you taste my ecstasy as I choke you with it."

With my free hand, I guide her much smaller hand down to my straining cock, wrapping her fingers around it. "Do you feel that, baby?" She nods slightly, gazing up at me through a thick haze of lust.

"You do this to me. It's all for you, but this shouldn't have happened because I don't want to get your hopes up. What I said I want is just that, a want, not a reality. I care for you too much to risk it." Dropping my hands from her, I step back from her grip, my dick twitching in protest. "I'll wait outside with Steve. Don't take too long."

Before she can utter one more word of protest, I leave the room, closing the door behind me and leaning against it with a shaky exhalation.

"What happened?" Steve asks, a knowing look on his features, the corner of his mouth twitching with barely restrained humor.

"Faun happened."

Steve just laughs boisterously and leans on the wall beside me, crossing his arms. "Doesn't she always?"

CHAPTER 14
FAUN

Venom and Steve walk me back to my room, where Nanuk and Sabre are waiting for me. I'm used to always having one of the guys with me as a guard, but lately, it just feels like I'm an unruly child being passed between parents, or even worse, like the prisoner that I am.

What happened in the bathroom was by far the sexiest thing I've ever experienced, but by the same token, it was also the most frustrating thing ever. I was so not done with Venom.

The reason they all have for staying away from me is stupid, and they're all wrong. They won't hurt me, and the very idea that they think they will, pisses me off.

I wish that masturbation helped to work off some of my heat, but it never does—if anything, it just adds fuel to the already burning inferno. Looking at the back of Venom's head, I sigh heavily. He won't even look at me now. I should probably be embarrassed, but I'm not. Being with these males feels so right to me, and I'm really over them fighting the pull that we have with each other.

Steve hands me off with a "good luck" to the others and a wink at me, and I can't help but smile at him. If given even a moment alone, he'd be all over me like butter on toast, so I'm not mad at him like the others.

"Well, what do you feel like doing?" Sabre asks in his rumbly, animalistic voice.

An idea comes to mind, and my eyes twinkle with excitement. "Since you two love a good competition, how about we go hang out in my room for some games? We can even make some bets." I use their competitive streak against them, and I can see it working instantly—these two never could say no to a fun gamble.

"I'm in. I haven't whipped that floor with this kitty cat in a while," Nanuk says excitedly as he rubs his hands together, opening my bedroom door and letting me enter first. "Poker?"

Sabre pushes himself in behind me before Nanuk gets a chance to walk through, a wide grin showing off all of his sharp teeth and not just his large saber teeth. "Get ready to lose more than just your pride, teddy bear."

"Ha! Fat chance," Nanuk laughs, grabbing the pack of cards from my bookcase and sitting at the end of my bed as I lean on the headboard after placing my discarded clothes and towel from earlier on the floor beside my bed. That's a later problem.

Sabre shakes his head and sits on the floor, facing us. "There's not enough room up there for all of us. Sit down here with me."

We follow him, but I mentally tell myself that I can make us all fit, and have to hide my smile. "What are we betting on, boys?" I ask, wanting them to relax into it before I try my luck with them.

I sit down and take my dressing gown off, throwing it behind me, revealing my green cami and bed shorts. I pretend not to notice Nanuk's gaze down my shirt as I lean over to pick up the cards he's dealing, or Sabre's laser focus on my long, crossed legs, the small material barely covering the junction between my thighs.

Sabre ruffles his scruffy ginger locks and fidgets in his seat as he takes his own cards, his eyes constantly flicking back to the origin of my heat.

"Um, how about if I win, I want a foot massage from Faun, and

Sabre, you must call me master for the rest of the week," Nanuk offers with an amused expression.

"Fine, but I want both of your puddings for a month," Sabre smirks, sure he's going to win.

I pretend like I'm thinking about something I want as I look at my three aces. I keep my face confused and scrunched up, when inside I'm soaring at the luck.

"Ah, I'm not sure. If I win..." I tap my chin, putting my cards down. "I'll pick the rules of the next game." Shrugging as though I can't think of something else, I yawn indifferently.

They both nod and Nanuk makes the first move, putting down three cards and picking up new ones, his eyes lighting up. "Get ready to rub my feet, pretty girl, because I've been on them all day."

Sabre scoffs and only changes one card in his deck, his face not changing, but the twinkle of victory colors his tiger's golden gaze.

I put down my pointless cards and receive two more, almost choking on my tongue at the fourth ace that appears before me, along with a three. I shake my head to cover up my shock and say, "That'll do."

"I'm good," Nanuk says, and Sabre agrees.

With an exaggerated flourish, Nanuk presents a straight with cards two to six. "Boom baby!"

Sabre laughs joyfully, throwing his own cards down. "Oh, too bad. Guess you won't be needing those puddings for a while."

Nanuk curses under his breath as I gingerly place down my four-of-a-kind, ace high, and ask dumbly, "Is this good?"

They both stare at my hand in shock, their eyes bugging out of their heads, and I let a giggle out. "Oh, yeah, that's right. I win, losers!" I pull the cards back together and pass them to Sabre. "You shuffle. Let's play strip poker, ladies' choice, remember?"

"I think we've been hustled, dude," Nanuk admits, sounding impressed despite losing. "Faun, this is a terrible idea."

"I didn't know you were a Broken chicken?" I ask sarcastically, clucking.

Without the slightest hesitation, Sabre shuffles the deck expertly, his eyes locked on mine. "I'm not sure if I want you to win or lose," he tells me honestly, and Nanuk grunts in agreement.

The next hand plays out quickly, everyone on edge with a thick tension in the air, and to my great enjoyment, I win again. Both males take off their shirts, leaving their combined peck hotness out on full display, but I've seen that a million times before. It's the next two hands I want to win.

Losing the next round to Nanuk because my hand is pure rubbish, Sabre takes his trousers off easily, his focus unwavering on me as I slowly grab the bottom of my cami shirt, lifting it above my head.

As soon as the cool air hits my exposed nipples, I hear two sharp inhales of breath, and I smile behind the curtain of fabric, then quickly seal my face again, so they can't see it.

I lean over, picking up the cards, pretending like it's totally normal for me to be as shirtless as they are, and start shuffling the cards. The slight movement of my hands makes my breasts jiggle and sway, capturing their undivided attention. I flick my gaze to Sabre's crotch quickly and almost moan at the rock-hard length, stretching out his underwear to the point that the thick bulbous head peeks over the top of the fabric.

Dishing out their new cards, I look down at my own, but am completely unfazed at what they are because I plan on folding anyway, determined to get naked as quickly as I can now. I clench my core in anticipation, and Nanuk sniffs the air and shivers.

They both swap some cards, and I place mine down and shrug. "Fold." The air feels as if it gets sucked from the room, but I don't move to undress. Instead, I lift my hand in a 'proceed' gesture.

"Right, um, I..." Sabre stutters and adjusts himself, trying to keep his not so little tiger in the small fabric he has left. "I have a full house." He places his cards on the floor between us, trying to look anywhere but at me.

Nanuk throws his three-of-a-kind down and curses. He stands up and drops his pants. To my absolute viewing pleasure, Nanuk went commando today, and he's now as naked as a babe.

My Cheshire grin spreads over my face as I stand before him and the still sitting Sabre. "It's only fair," I practically purr, wiggling my bed shorts down to reveal my own lack of panties. "You know, I can think of something else we can do to pass the time."

Dropping back down to my knees before Nanuk, right in front of his hard cock, I lick my lips and look slyly at Sabre with a wink as I lick it from the base to the tip, his salty skin so tasty that I groan. My need skyrockets to an immeasurable level.

I always wondered what this would taste like.

CHAPTER 15
NANUK

"Fuck."

My mind feels like it explodes the second her warm, soft, wet tongue glides along my length and my eyes roll into the back of my head. "Do that again," I plead, needing more.

Suddenly the tip of my dick is buried in heaven, and I look down to find Faun's perfect lips wrapped around me, and I almost cum there and then. She locks eyes with me and bobs her head up and down, sucking and tasting me, a look of pure enjoyment on her face like it's the best thing she's ever tasted, and I growl deep in my throat.

I give up on not touching her when she takes me even deeper into her throat, slightly gagging on my size. My large hands grab her antlers at the base savagely, and my hips thrust forward of their own volition as I start to fuck her face, needing more. And by God, she happily takes her small hands and grasps my hips, encouraging me to keep going.

"That's the hottest thing I've ever seen," Sabre growls beside Faun, and I hazily watch as his fingers dip between her legs. "I fucking love your tail. It's sexy as fuck."

Faun moans so deep that it vibrates up my shaft, and I clench my teeth, not wanting to cum yet. As I fuck her face, I look down to see a small fluffy tail twitching above her ass crack, and it's cute as hell. Faun keeps moaning and grinding herself into Sabre's hand, who greedily watches every move she makes, openly stroking himself through his pants at the same time.

As another violent vibration rips up my shaft, I pull my hips back, knowing I'm not going to make it inside her if I don't, and I've gone way too far to stop now.

Reading my mind, Faun moves Sabre's hand and stands up, moving to the bed backward with a come here motion with her finger, and we both follow her like the pied piper. Her pussy, the flute.

She sits back on the bed and scoots back. I grab her ankles and twist her so that she has to go on her stomach, and then raise her knees up on the bed and marvel at her wet pussy on show as her ass and tail are up in the air.

Sabre stalks around her with hungry eyes, dropping his underwear as he goes and sliding in front of her with his dick in his hand, the command in his eyes obvious, and she acquiesces with pleasure.

I rub my hands over Faun's smooth golden globes as I watch Sabre's mouth round in ecstasy as she bobs her head up and down on him, groaning with delight the whole time.

"It's better than you thought, isn't it?" I ask him, with Sabre's only answer, a guttural groan of appreciation.

My focus moves to Faun's sweet spot and I bend down closer— it's more beautiful than I ever imagined. I've seen them in porn and stuff, but it's so much more *everything* in person.

Leaning in, I taste the juices licking tentatively, and I'm shocked at how delicious her pussy is. It's like nothing I've ever tasted before— somehow sweet and yet buttery—and I plan on never having a day without this on my tongue again.

"You've got to try this," I mumble as I nuzzle into the wet flesh, covering my face with it.

Faun lets go of Sabre's dick with a popping sound and turns to look at me over her shoulder. "You have to gently massage the clit. It's the button bit, and I like fingers inside me at the same time too," she tells me informatively, which is great because otherwise, I'd probably just stay down here devouring her without any actual direction.

I chuckle quietly about all the movies that talk about human men not knowing how to do this, before I start using my tongue on the area she told me to. I'm rewarded with a mewling sound, her hips arching further. *Yep, that must be the place.*

I go to put my finger inside her, but then remember my wicked long claws. *Maybe not.* I massage my tongue against her clit and watch her body for cues on what she does and doesn't like, and way sooner than I expect, she climaxes, supplying me with a fresh wave of deliciousness.

Her cries echo through the room and I know they're going to be addictive, my male pride growing at bringing her so much joy with just my tongue.

Kneeling behind her, I rub my cock up and down soaking folds, groaning as I do, and look over to find Sabre's hooded eyes watching me as he strokes Faun's antlers lovingly while she sucks his cock. I can see in his eyes that he doesn't want to miss the moment I slip inside her.

I nudge the head of my cock at her entrance and feel briefly confused about how it's meant to fit in such a small hole. "Will I fit in there?" I ask. "I don't want to hurt you."

Faun stops using her mouth and looks back at me, wiggling her ass with need. "Please Nanuk, it's meant to hurt the first few times I think, but the pain can't be worse than I'm already feeling. Please, don't stop. I can handle it."

I look at Sabre, fear in my heart at our difference in size, and he nods in understanding, happy to take over for me. As much as I would love to be the first male inside her, I'm quite a bit bigger than normal because of my size. At least I'm not beast-size like Ironside. There's no way he's going to fit in there.

"Faun, sweetheart, lie on your back. I'm going to take control now, okay?" Sabre tells her softly but with a firm tone, brokering no argument as he moves off the bed. She nods in agreement, moving her body to lie back on the bed, opening her legs for us in invitation.

With a smirk, he looks down at her like it's Christmas morning and begins crawling up the bed, between her legs, stopping at her core and snarling in a hunger I understand well.

Bending down, he uses his large tongue to lick up her new juices, and Faun wriggles on the bed, panting in need. "Please," she begs, and he relents, crawling the rest of the way up her body, nuzzling her neck with love as only a Broken feline would.

Sabre leans up and asks, "Are you sure?" She answers with a breathy "Yes," and he reaches down, grasping his cock, and starts to slowly maneuver it inside her. Faun's eyes open wider in pain, and I decide to help, moving to the side of the bed and slipping my hands between their bodies.

With careful, slick movements, I start to rub her little nub the same way I did with my mouth earlier, and it helps almost straight away. Sabre keeps pushing slowly inside her, but Faun seems to relax marginally, arching her hips to my dedicated touch.

A small cry mixed with both pleasure and pain leaves her parted lips, and Sabre quickly pushes the rest of the way in. I keep up my ministrations as he stops moving, letting Faun become adjusted to the new large object filling her most delicate area.

Her breathing starts to hitch and her hips arch so high that she begins to shake, chasing her building orgasm, and when it hits, she screams, her head back and eyes squeezed closed.

Sabre starts to slowly move while she's riding her high and the scent of blood tinges the air, making him stop, and we move to stare down at her in horror.

"Keep going," she mewls through her mix of pleasure and pain.

Sabre and I look at each other in worry, but he slowly begins moving again, fear still partially stamped on his face. With each movement, her moans become less filled with pain and more with need.

"More, harder," Faun mewls, her little nails digging into Sabre's back. And I've never been more jealous of anyone in my whole life, but I know I've done the right thing.

Their tempo increases, and my dick twitches at how fucking hot it is. Grabbing myself, I start stroking in time with their thrusts, my own panting getting hot and heavy.

"I can't hold on," Sabre growls between his teeth, reaching up to hold on to her antlers to pull himself deeper, and she loves it.

"Don't stop. Don't stop. Oh, God. Don't. Stop," Faun cries out, lost in her need.

Sabre starts fucking her wildly, letting his beast out a little, but not enough to seriously hurt her. They hit a crescendo, and the second she starts to scream out with her thighs squeezing the life out of him, Sabre joins her, growling into her throat and bucking his hips wildly.

I squeeze the tip of my dick, trying not to cum all over them because I need to lose my load inside her. If she'll let me.

Tapping Sabre's back, he rolls his head up to look at me with utter satisfaction on his face. "Move, or you're about to get sticky as fuck, bro," I grind out.

"Can I?" I ask Faun, with her cheeks flushed and hair a crazy mess around her antlers.

Sabre grunts at me, unhappy that I've asked him to move, but does it anyway, although reluctantly, and Faun reaches up to embrace me.

"Get down here," she demands with a smile, and my heart leaps, knowing that she wants me too.

With a flash of movement, I slide between her strong, sleek thighs and nudge the head of my cock inside her without a pause. Her channel still feels really tight, but I feel a lot more confident now than I did before. "Can you take me, pretty girl?" I ask, making sure.

"Fuck yes," she moans, grabbing my ass and pulling me in deeper.

I groan into her hair at the feeling of her slick heat. "You feel perfect." I roll my hips to show her just how perfect she feels, filling her to the brim.

Not able to stop now that I've started, I hold her body close to mine and thrust into her again and again, feeling her little body trembling below me. Moving my hand between her, I repeat what I learned earlier about her body and almost instantly, she starts to come undone again. *Holy shit, this thing is powerful.*

With her cries in my ear, legs around my back, and pussy strangling my dick, I cum deep inside the love of my life and know this moment couldn't be any more perfect.

CHAPTER 16
STEVE

"Guys, you wouldn't believe what I saw," I say through my laughter as I fling open Faun's door and stroll inside.

The scene before me freezes, and my eyes bulge so much that they feel like they might fall right out of my head.

When I came in here, not once did I think I'd find a naked Sabre standing over an equally naked Nanuk, balls deep in Faun. *Holy fuck. What did I miss?*

Faun's long golden legs are wrapped tightly around Nanuk as they both stare at me, shocked, and no shit, it's funny as hell. I crack up laughing, my body bent over and my boisterous laugh carrying down the hall behind me.

Sabre runs over and slams the door behind me to keep a semblance of privacy, and it just makes me laugh even harder. He smacks the back of my head and grumbles his way over to put his pants on.

"It's not that funny, dude," Nanuk grumbles, getting up off Faun and carefully covering her with her blanket.

Sabre's fully dressed by the time Nanuk has his own pants on, and I've calmed down enough to get words out. "This is absolute gold. I can't wait to tell Mayne. He's gonna shit a brick." I clap my hands as if they'd put on a good show for me. "Bravo boys."

"Shut the fuck up. You're gonna upset Faun," Sabre growls at me, looking like he's about to pounce on me at any moment, but when I look over at the bed, I instantly spot Faun trying to cover her own amusement with her blankets.

"So," I say, moving over to her and sitting on the end of the bed, leaning back and looking at the two flustered males before me. "Did you hurt her? Is Faun in dire need of a doctor, or was I right all along?" I ask, smug as fuck because clearly a good time was had by all, and I'm shockingly not the slightest bit jealous. "It's okay to admit that I am all-knowing."

Faun giggles behind me, and I turn to give her a cheeky wink.

"I think we should talk in the hallway for a minute, Steve," Nanuk says, and I suppress a growl. How hard is it to call me Crush?

"That's an excellent idea, bro," I answer, instead of biting back about my name, again. I look at Faun. "Give me a second. I won't be long. Well, I will be long, but not in time." I wink again and bounce off the bed with my arms open wide, directing the other two to the door with me.

Sabre and Nanuk move out into the hall ahead of me, and I lean on the doorjamb with a smile. "Enjoy your talk, fellas. I've got a date with a carnal embrace."

Before they can react, I slam the door in their faces and lock it. I turn with a huge smile and bound back on the bed, laughing as I bounce with it, then crawl up Faun's body, licking my lips. "Where were we? Oh yeah, you were about to ride the bony express."

Faun laughs out loud and wraps her arms around my neck, pulling me in and kissing the tip of my nose, while dumb and dumber pound on the door.

"You're feeling extra cheeky today," she tells me softly, a glint of excitement in her eyes.

I snort a laugh. "Are you kidding? This is the best day of my life," I say, slowly pulling the blankets off her, exposing every inch of her magnificent body. "They may have broken the rules for me, but you're all mine now, and I'm never letting you go again."

Faun's eyes soften as she looks up at me and then pulls me down again, kissing me softly but passionately, and the whole world melts away as I let her claim me for her own with her delicate lips. I drown in her taste and I love it.

As much as I crave to be inside her, I know that it's a lot to ask of someone who is new to this, especially after already being stretched by my pack brothers.

"I can wait as long as you need me to," I whisper against her lips in between our kisses.

Without warning, Faun flips me over with strength I didn't realize she had, and climbs on my lap, straddling me. The visual feast is enough to make me groan and almost cum in my pants. Her long, shapely body is on full display, and her pussy is open and swollen as she grinds herself against my straining, confined cock.

"You better not make me wait for a second longer, Steve. I've been wanting you inside me for more time than I'm comfortable with," she complains, still rolling her hips.

Her heat must be intense if she's already wanting more sex. Good thing she has a whole pack to keep her busy. I chuckle at the thought and grab her hips, lifting her higher.

"You're gonna have to let me take my pants off," I say with a side smile, not one word of objection on my lips, because she's not the only one that's been wanting this.

Instead of moving away, Faun reaches down and undoes my zipper, before dipping into my pants, grabbing my cock with her hand, and squeezing.

"Fuck that," she complains and pulls it out, while I groan at the feel of her skin against me there.

In a swift movement, she starts to lower herself down onto my hard length. My head pushes back on the pillow and a guttural moan leaves my lips because her wet heat feels so fucking good as it strangles my cock.

It takes a bit of maneuvering for her to get fully seated, and it is by far the best fucking thing I've ever felt in my life. I knew it would be incredible, but I had no idea that anything could feel this good.

"Fuck me, it's all yours," I tell her through clenched teeth, dying for her to move.

I want Faun to have full control over me for a change. Tonight I'm her prey and she can do whatever she wants with me because I want her to know that she holds all the power.

With slow, steady movements, Faun starts to ride me, her wet pussy swallowing me whole over and over again. The slow pace is enough to drive me mad, and it takes all of my restraint to let her be in charge. My eyes squeeze tightly closed, and my fingers clench against her hips, and she chuckles.

I snap my eyes open to look up at her smirk. "You really are going to let me do what I want, aren't you? Do you want me to fuck you harder? Faster?" Her voice comes out breathy, her cheeks pink with pleasure.

"Yes. Please," I growl, needing it, but willing to let her decide.

Faun leans over me, pulling my shirt up to my chin, and then rubbing her taut nipples along my exposed chest. "Kiss me, big guy. Let's get sweaty."

Her lips crash against mine at the same time that her hips start pounding down on me hard and fast. My hands grab her tight ass to help her to connect with me rougher as I lift my hips to meet hers, deciding instantly to ignore the fur I touch. The feeling of filling her tight confine in this angle has me panting and trying not to blow my load too quickly.

Our kiss is harsh and messy, our teeth clashing with our growing need. The friction of my body against her pussy makes her movements more frantic, and her breathing hitches before she groans in my mouth, her body shaking around me as her cunt clasps me so tight it practically forces my cum into her. My orgasm is so violent that black dots flash over my vision and I feel like I almost black out.

We lay sweaty and panting in each other's arms, not saying a word for the longest time, and I let my body relax into the moment, enjoying having Faun draped over me like the perfect blanket.

A few minutes pass, and I'm stunned to realize that Faun is fast asleep, her body limp and trusting as her soft breaths tickle my cheek. Hopefully, she doesn't move suddenly because her antlers gauging out one of my eyes would be a real buzz kill.

I gently stroke my fingers up and down her spine, trying to tattoo this memory into my head forever because I don't want to forget a single second of my time alone with her. I hope to God that this changes everything because I don't know if I could ever go back to the way things were before.

My brow crinkles in worry when I think about everything that we've been keeping from her regarding what happened with Dr. Micheals and Antonio. It didn't feel right hiding it all from her before, and it feels even worse now.

Regardless of what the others believe, I'm going to fight them on this, and if they don't agree, well, tough shit, because I'll be telling her everything anyway, with or without them.

A tiny moan comes from Faun's parted lips, and I wonder if she's dreaming about what we just did together. I hope this meant as much to her as it did to me. I suppose only time will tell.

The silence around me gets broken by the sound of someone picking the lock on Faun's door. I tense at the idea that it might mean someone wanting to do her harm, but it's much more likely to be one of my pack mates pissed off that I locked them out.

I'm not sure when Nanuk and Sabre stopped banging on the door earlier because I had way more pressing matters at the time—like claiming my female—but I guess they eventually took off when they heard the noises we were no doubt making.

Faun's door opens slowly and my body relaxes when Venom and Tallon poke their heads in, their eyes instantly locking on Faun's exposed ass.

Not liking the idea of people ogling her without her consent or knowledge, I carefully cover us up with the previously discarded blankets and give them both a slightly smug smile; because there's no way that they don't wish they were me right now. I give myself a mental note to ask her later on about that adorable little tail she never told us about.

"Is she okay?" Tallon asks, his eyes traveling over her with concern, obviously worried that one of us may have hurt her.

Happy to reassure him, because it's a fear that we'd all held for such a long time, I give a swift nod and thumbs up.

Tallon puffs out a relieved sigh and backs out of the room, while Venom continues to linger in the doorway. "Are you okay to stay in here tonight, or do you want to swap?" he asks, envy and longing in his eyes.

Fuck that shit. I'm nice, but I'm not that nice. I flip him the bird and point to the door, indicating that I want him to leave. He gives me the finger back but smiles in understanding, backing out and closing the door behind him, leaving me alone with Faun for the night for the first—but hopefully not the last—time.

I close my eyes, inhale her sweet, woodsy scent and snuggle her closer to me. "Sweet dreams. I love you," I whisper to her, kissing her temple tenderly, and letting sleep take me.

CHAPTER 17
FAUN

I PULL MY SHOULDERS BACK AND STALK INTO MAYNE'S ROOM with my best 'don't fuck with me' face, ready for war if he wants to start shit about me hooking up with Nanuk, Steve, and Sabre yesterday.

I'm not sure why we were all called in here for a pack meeting, but my guess is Mayne's dissatisfaction over what happened, and I'm not going to let him or any of the others tell me what I can and can't do with my body now that I know what I'll be missing out on.

"Stand down, soldier," Alfa says to me with amusement, reading my hard expression. "You're not here for a fight, so relax a little."

As the last of us join our little tête-à-tête, I brace myself when Mayne turns his full attention on me. *I freaking knew it.* I barely manage to stop my eyes from rolling at his stern expression.

"Get on with it then," I grumble, frustrated because I'm over this shit now. It's been going on too long, and I refuse to let anyone make me feel guilty or worried about my sexual needs. I'm a grown-ass woman and I know what I want.

Mayne rubs his face, seeming agitated, and sits on the end of his bed before leaning on his elbows and looking up at me. "I'm sorry, beautiful," he starts, and my jaw drops open. I didn't even know he knew that word. "I wish that when I called a meeting, you didn't automatically assume it's because I'm going to attack or berate you over something, and that's on me. I'm not sorry for wanting to protect you, and I'm not going to say I'm not still concerned, but at the end of the day, it's your choice who you choose to take to your bed. Just be careful."

"As much as I appreciate the sentiment, my sex life should never be the item of topic in a pack meeting," I retort, not unkindly but with enough force that it's clear that I'm done with this being an issue.

"Noted and agreed." Mayne nods once. "Now, to the actual reason we're here. You're not going to be happy about this, but it needs to be said if we're going to keep peace within our pack." His gaze slides to Steve, who has his arms crossed and a smug look on his face.

What's that about?

"Recently, Tallon came across a very serious conversation between Dr. Micheals and Antonio that has changed everything as we know it," Mayne starts, his focus now fully on me. "Before you get all pissed off with us for not telling you straight away, please remember that we were doing it so that you could feel at peace as long as possible. There's no way to sugarcoat this. They are planning on killing all of us and starting their experiment again from scratch."

My heart stops, and the room seems to shrink in on me. The only noise I can make out is the beating of my heart inside my head. *Kill us? Why?*

A hand on my shoulder has me jumping out of my skin, and I turn with wide eyes to see Styng looking down at me with a concerned gaze. "I've got you, baby. Just breathe."

I hadn't realized that I was holding my breath until he mentions it, and I let it go with a heavy whoosh. "When?" I croak out, looking back at Mayne, his nervous appearance now making a lot more sense.

"It seems they're having a meeting to discuss it sometime in the next month or so," he tells me tiredly. "Ironside went and had a talk with both the Dr. Adina's, and they appear to be on our side and are looking into alternative avenues to keep us safe, but honestly, I don't know how much stock to put in that."

Ironside steps forward with his arms wide. "They were really concerned. I think we can trust them."

"Regardless, we need to come up with our own plan to escape if you ask me," Mayne adds.

My mind goes back to Morigan saying I could always go to her and how I've always felt that I can trust her. "Let me go and see Morigan and see what she can tell me. When was the last time anyone talked to her?" I ask, looking between the males around me.

"It's been a couple of weeks," Styng chimes in. "It couldn't hurt. Plus, you two seem to have forged some kind of friendship over the years."

I nod, agreeing. "Tell me everything you know." I listen attentively to all the details and try my hardest not to panic.

Morigan takes one look at my face when the door closes and says, "So, they finally told you, did they?"

"Why didn't you tell me?" I ask in return, feeling a slight twinge of betrayal because I was really beginning to see her as my friend and not just my doctor.

With a sigh, she takes her normal seat. "I wanted to, but dad told me not to get in between pack politics, and I didn't want to cause any more issues amid you and the guys than you were already dealing with. Speaking of, how is all that stuff going? Did any of them put out yet?"

"Nope," I say, popping my p and sitting down heavily, crossing my arms. "We're not doing that. You're going to be honest with me about what's going on, and if I'm satisfied that you're not lying to me, then we can talk about other shit."

Morigan nods her head sadly. "Fair enough. You should know

that we are doing everything we can to convince the board that your lives are valuable, and that to terminate phase one would be a huge mistake, not to mention immoral."

"What are the chances that they're going to listen to you two?" I ask, needing to know.

With a nervous shuffle in her seat, Morigan replies honestly, "Not great, but that won't stop us from trying. In the meantime, though, we've been working on a backup plan. Actually, my dad has had this avenue in the back of his mind since not long after you were born. I can't give you too much detail because I only know so much, and I don't want to get your hopes up. Then there's also the issue of how on earth we would be able to enact a plan like that. There are a lot of reasons why getting you all out of here is anything but simple, and the security here is nothing to laugh at."

It makes sense that she wouldn't be able to tell me everything, especially since there's nothing any of us can do to help them from inside these walls. But I'm grateful she's attempting to tell me what she can, and I do trust her, even if I probably shouldn't.

"Even if you do manage to get us out of here, how are humans going to take us running around free? Won't we be hunted? What if some of the others, like Sylva, go out hunting humans instead?" I ask, my mind running a mile a minute at all the possible outcomes, and none of them seems to be a good one. As much as I want to live free, I don't want to do it if it means risking those I love or the lives of all the innocent people that wouldn't be prepared for the Broken predators that live here.

"That's some of the many problems that we're trying to sort out," Morigan agrees. "If we manage to get you and your pack out, Faun, it will only be the ten of you because while I don't believe it's right to terminate anyone, I can't be responsible for the potential destruction that others could reign down on the human race. It's not a choice that I'll live with lightly, but I hope you don't judge me too harshly for it."

I really don't because she's right. It doesn't stop me from feeling sick in the pit of my stomach, though.

"Is there anywhere that we would even be safe out there? What will we even do?" I ask, more nervous about my future than I ever have been before.

Morigan licks her lips and looks around the room as if she's trying to find an answer, but her eyes harden as she comes to some kind of decision. "I'm going to tell you something that I really shouldn't, but you have a right to know because I want you to have hope. My father bought an island a very long time ago that's pretty far off the radar. He did it so that if a day like this came, he would have a safe refuge for you. It's unoccupied and has no utilities on it, and never will either if we want to keep it secret. He started rumors a long time ago about how it's riddled with poisonous snakes, carnivorous ants, and a myriad of other things that people want to avoid. The whole island is clearly marked all the way around with danger signs and warnings, and so far it's been completely left alone. Over the years, we have added new animal species to grow and thrive, as well as planted a good mix of edible plants, fruit trees, and anything else you might need to live off the land. If all goes well, it will be a safe haven for you and your pack, but it will be a much rougher life than you're used to, and you will not be able to leave."

I let everything she's telling me roll around in my head, and my fear slowly ebbs, making room for anticipation and the first-ever hope I've had for freedom. These two people have spent their lives preparing a safe haven for us, even though they had no way to know if there was going to be any of us worth saving, and my appreciation for them skyrockets.

Tears sting my eyes as I look at her, my lip trembling violently. A stray droplet escapes as I whisper, "Thank you."

Morigan jumps up from her seat, kneels before me, and wraps her arms around me tightly, holding me close as a sob escapes me, and I'm shocked to find her own shoulders shaking with sobs along with mine.

We spend the next few minutes crying on each other's shoulders, our tears flowing freely and our bond further strengthening, as the severity and fragility of our situation thicken the air.

Sitting back and wiping her wet eyes, Morigan smiles at me softly. "You never have to thank me for this, Faun. You should never have been in this situation to begin with, and as long as I live, I will fight for your freedom. We don't have a lot to offer, and the island isn't ideal, but it's what we could do with the situation we're in; and it seems to be the only way we can guarantee your safety from human prying eyes."

"It's everything. Even if something happens, and we don't make it there one day, I want you to know how grateful I am. You're the closest thing I have to a sister, and it means the world to me," I tell her, needing her to know how much everything they're doing matters.

A knock sounds on the door, reminding us that I've been in here too long. "You okay in there, Dr. Adina?" the guard of the day asks through the door.

"Yes, thank you. We'll only be a few more minutes," she replies loud enough for him to hear before she lowers her voice again. "Remember, be careful where you talk about this with your pack, and don't trust anyone else. It's pivotal that this remains confidential."

I agree wholeheartedly, and there's no way I'd risk this getting out. It may be our only hope for not only freedom but also to survive the year.

I get up and start walking toward the door when Morigan grabs my arm. "You didn't tell me about what's happening with your heat issue," she says, tilting her head in curiosity.

With a huge grin, I say, "Oh, that's being taken care of now." I can't help the giggle that slips out.

"Nooo. Who?" she practically squeals.

"So far only three, but I'm working on the rest," I joke, and her eyes go as wide as saucers. "I'll give you all the goss' next time, I promise."

With a loud laugh, she says, "You'd better," before opening the door. I leave feeling a hell of a lot better than I did when I arrived.

CHAPTER 18
TALLON

As Faun sits down on the edge of my bed next to Ironside and tells us everything that she and Dr. Adina talked about, I can't help but admire the ethereal creature before me even more than I did before.

Even though Faun is undoubtedly rattled by this new development, she's holding her head high and dealing with it head-on. It's hard to believe she was made from prey sometimes; her human half must have strong genes to have turned out such a woman.

"I can't believe we could be free of this place," she says softly, her eyes far away in dreams of a new land. "I never really thought I'd leave the Ark, at least not alive."

A truer statement was never said. It's not as if we linger on our existence here with much tenacity because we understand our place in the grand scheme of things, but it's always in the back of our minds, a shadow that never fades.

Before I let my somber thoughts press on me too hard, I smile at Faun and say, "We'll have to scavenge for food like the travelers of afore. I can imagine it now, us men chopping down the trees and building suitable lodging, while you wear a coconut bra and lie in the sun bossing us around."

Alfa, Styng, and Steve snigger, but Faun stands up and places her tight fists on her hips with a harrumph. "Excuse you, Tallon. I'll have you know that I'm more than likely going to be running and swimming in the sea as I oversee your work with great enthusiasm." The twinkle in her eye grows as she smiles wide, enjoying the game.

"No. No. No," Ironside booms playfully, shaking his head. "No woman of mine will be frolicking in the waves while I'm working up a big appetite. You'll be at the fire, cooking me a seafood feast."

Faun playfully swats his chest, rolling her eyes. "In your dreams, big guy."

"Every night. Amongst other things," he growls, grabbing her by her tiny waist and hoisting her on his lap.

With a comfort and ease that soothes my soul, she snuggles into his unnecessarily wide chest and sighs.

The new development of our group dynamic is everything I've always wanted. Deep in my heart, I knew I would never hurt her, not just because I'm much less of a threat to her than my pack brothers, but also because there's not a single part of me that could. The reason I went along with the pact was purely that it didn't seem right to embrace a love we should all be sharing, and I knew someday they would overcome their fear and find faith in themselves to love Faun freely.

We all haven't taken those first steps, but it's just a matter of time now, and it's an unspoken thing that she's now ours fully, as much as we are hers, if anything, more so.

"Let's be honest here," Sabre says, playing with the tips of Faun's antlers while looking down at her lovingly. "Faun will end up as the chief of our little village, and we will merely be her humble servants, ready to please her in any way she deems fit."

Her cheeks pinken with his illustrious words of worship, and the blushing tinge of her golden skin makes her even more beautiful.

"All hail, chief Faun," Styng cries out, and we chorus him merrily, loving the look of tender adoration that dawns on her precious face.

We laugh together and play along for what seems like hours until adjourning to our own rooms one by one, except for Faun, who stands near the door shuffling her feet nervously.

"What's wrong, precious?" I ask, stroking one hand down her silky smooth arm. "You seem out of sorts."

Faun's beautiful eyes look up at me with longing and sadness. "Can I stay with you tonight?" Her question stops my heart, and I have to force myself to breathe, hoping she didn't notice. "I know that it looks like everything's going to be okay, but I have terrible nightmares, and I don't want to be alone anymore."

I pull her into my embrace, holding her tight and secure as I kiss her temple and whisper, "You never have to ask, precious. Everything that is mine is yours, and I'd be honored to keep you safe in your sleep."

Her tight shoulders slump and she relaxes into me, her small arms wrapping around my waist. "I knew you wouldn't judge me."

"Never. I'm here for you anytime you need me, just like you were there for me," I respond into her hair, careful not to take my eye out with her antler. They're a real pain in the butt sometimes, even if they are beautiful.

Faun looks up at me with a vulnerable look on her face. "Be honest, is that the only reason I'm in this pack?"

If she had asked me that when we first invited her to become one of us, I would have told her yes because it was the truth. I owed this girl my life. Without her sitting by my side after my wings were brutally taken from me, I would have ended my existence because without them, I was lost, and life without them was too much to bear.

Sometimes, I still feel my missing limbs like an ache I can never soothe, or an itch I can never scratch, but every time the darkness of their loss threatens to drown me in pain and bitterness, my beautiful Faun smiles up at me and takes my hand. Somehow, always aware when I need her the most.

Now, though, she is so much more than my savior. She is my friend, my family, and my heart. The truth is not what it once was and as I look at her searching gaze, I answer with all of my heart. "You're a part of our pack because we can't live without you. Because we love you and you belong with us. You're my home, Faun; wherever you are, I am too."

FAUN

Home? That's a damn good answer, but I should have expected nothing less from my most eloquent of males.

"You're my home too." I know it's not the fanciest answer, but it's an honest one, and I know he'll appreciate it all the same.

Feeling brazen and super lovey-dovey after Tallon wooing my heart so successfully, a need to be closer to him overcomes me, and I reach up on my tiptoes and kiss his lips as sweetly as I can, tasting him and taking my time without devouring him.

"Will you make love to me, Tallon? I need you," I ask, letting my vulnerability take a step back and going for what I want.

Without missing a beat, Tallon kisses me again, pulling me tighter against him and stepping forward so I have no choice but to keep stepping back, trusting in his guidance.

The back of my knees hit the edge of his bed and instead of pushing me down, he steps back from me, putting unwanted distance between our bodies. Before I can protest, he whips his shirt off, leaving his impressive chest bare for my ogling pleasure.

Tallon is barely seen without a shirt covering him because of the malformed scars lining his back. The reminder they bring is always too much for him to handle, and his move surprises me.

With a deep breath, Tallon says to me, "Will you accept me with these?" He turns his now stiff body and faces away, leaving me with the full view of his devastation. If I could kill Antonio for doing this to him, I would. To this day, that prick still openly mocks Tallon about it and jokes on his behalf, uncaring of the pain it inflicts, or more likely *because* of it.

Stepping forward, I tenderly touch the top of both scars with my fingers, and tears spring to my eyes as he flinches at the simple contact but doesn't move away.

I lean in and gently kiss the top of his left scar before trailing down it slowly, kissing every single inch with love and reverence, before repeating the process with the right side. By the time I'm done, silent tears have soaked my face, and Tallon's strong body trembles, but with what I'm not sure.

"I not only accept you, but I love you just the way you are, and I never want you to hide these from me again," I say, wetting his back with my tears as I wrap my arms around him.

Tallon turns in my arms, grasping my cheeks with both of his hands, and kisses me, harder this time. With gentle movements, he lays me down on the bed and strips me down to my skin.

"Can I?" he asks me, his voice huskier than normal and all I can do is nod as he slips the pants from his body, then kneels at my feet.

He licks, kisses, and nips at every bit of my skin, making me moist with need and tremble all over. By the time he makes it to my core, I'm practically vibrating. "Please?" I beg, wanting his mouth where it really counts.

Lowering his mouth, I feel Tallon's now hot breath across my wet pussy lips, and let out a small moan. "Please, what? What do you want? Tell me precious?"

"I want you to kiss me here," I say, moving my fingers down my body to circle my swollen nub and glide between my lips.

Tallon curses under his breath and moves my hand suddenly, diving in like a man possessed, and to my delight, it takes me less than a minute to climax. The build-up was so fierce that I came like a rocket, seeing stars.

Before I can see straight, Tallon thrusts inside me without warning, and I cry out again. The sensation of being so full is like coming home.

We move together in perfect harmony, our gazes locked and breathing each other's air. The way we connect together is immovable and something that you'd read out of a book.

There's nothing rushed about our lovemaking, it's just pure emotion, filled with everything that our words can never say but our hearts long to.

We ride our high together, climbing and then collapsing as one. Tallon rolls to the side, taking me with him without losing our connection. He carefully fluffs the pillows under me so I can lie comfortably with my antlers, and kisses my eyes gently.

"Go to sleep, precious love. I'll protect you from bad dreams and keep you warm. I love you," Tallon tells me as my eyelids get too heavy to hold open. I whisper, "I love you too," before sleep takes me, and not one nightmare can be found.

CHAPTER 19
FAUN

My cheek rubs against a smooth chest, and I nuzzle into it. Stroking my hands up and down, I'm surprised to find no hair or bumps whatsoever—just soft, sleek skin—and I know what I'm going to find before I even open my eyes.

Venom has a very particular body; it is shiny black, almost like a shell. I guide my hands up to the middle of his chest and let my eyes open slowly, looking directly at the deep red hourglass that distinguishes his Broken species.

"Good morning, Spider-Man," I whisper into his skin, kissing his pec softly. "To what do I owe the pleasure?"

A large, rough hand comes around my hips, dipping down to cup my mound firmly. "Did someone say pleasure?" Alfa growls in my ear from behind as he grinds his body against mine provocatively, instantly waking up the rest of my mind. Venom just stares down at me with longing in his eyes, ever the talkative one.

"I must be lucky this morning. Where's Tallon?" I ask, pulling Alfa in closer with one arm behind me, while still snuggling into Venom.

Venom chuckles and Alfa says, "That's the point, my love. Tallon has an appointment this morning with one of the quacks about some eye test. He'll be back after, but in the meantime," he nips at my earlobe. "I want to talk more about you getting lucky."

Venom pulls me on top of his—apparently naked—body, and I slide myself along his length while taking his bottom lip into my mouth and nipping it softly.

"With pleasure," I moan, rolling against Venom again, and Alfa chuckles at my pun. I knew he'd like that.

Alfa pulls the blanket off us all, dropping it unceremoniously to the ground. "When were you going to tell us about this?" Alfa asks, stroking my sensitive tail.

I shiver and look back at him straddling Venom's legs behind me, his gaze firmly on my small tail. "When you earned it."

"Touché."

I resume kissing Venom, enjoying being so close to the silent but deadly male, his kisses more tentative than the others, no doubt worried about accidentally nipping me with his poisonous fangs.

Alfa's hand reaches between us, and he slides one finger into my already wet pussy. "You're so tight, love."

He adds another finger, stretching me out more, but it feels so damn good as I rub my clit up and down Venom's cock, coating him in my juices.

I feel his body move closer to mine, but I stay focused on kissing Venom, wanting him to feel comfortable with me so close to his deadliest feature, needing to show him that he won't hurt me.

The head of Alfa's cock nudges at my entrance straight after he takes out his large digits, and I look down at Venom. "Do you mind?" I ask because he might not appreciate me fucking someone else on top of him.

His dark eyes travel my face, and he smiles up at me. "I insist," he all but growls, looking behind me. "Fuck her hard. I want Faun to cum all over me."

Holy shit. That's not what I was expecting him to say, but it turned me the fuck on.

My pussy practically gushes with excitement as Alfa fills me, thrusting in and out in a hard but steady rhythm that I get lost in. Crying out as he fucks me, while Venom caresses me all over before moving his hand to my clit, and circling my wetness around it, just the way I showed him in the bathroom that time, driving me insane.

Just before I climax, they both stop and Alfa pulls out of me. "What the fuck?" I growl, super pissed off all of a sudden.

My anger doesn't last long as Venom takes Alfa's place, filling me back up and moaning deeply. "Oh my God, you feel good."

Alfa stays quiet but starts rubbing his soaked dick up and down between my ass cheeks, randomly pushing gently on my back hole, and it feels way better than I thought something like that would.

My orgasm starts to build again, and Alfa pushes the head of his cock a little harder against my back entrance. I could tell him to stop, but I don't want to. It feels too freaking good.

Venom reaches between us and pays attention to my clit again as Alfa works on slowly stretching me open from behind. The mixture of sensations skyrockets my release and I cry out, pushing my hips back, needing more, and Alfa slides in with a deep growl.

My body shakes with pleasurable tremors and they both start to fuck me in sync, slow but deep, and before my climax fully stops another one rolls over me, and I cum even harder than the first time, screaming out and biting Venom's pec hard at the intense feeling.

I can feel my body gushing, and I momentarily wonder if I wet myself, but the thought is gone almost instantly as they pick up speed, miraculously staying in sync the whole time. Harder. Faster. Deeper. I get lost in the feeling, but I have no doubt that between the noises all three of us are making, the entire compound knows what we're doing.

A different grunting grabs my attention before I cum again, and I turn my head to find Tallon jerking off beside us, ready to blow.

My eyes roll into the back of my head, and I practically pass out as I peak again, taking both Venom and Alfa with me, filling me in both my holes. My ass seems to stretch even wider as Alfa's dick grows.

Tallon groans, and I lean over and open my mouth just in time, and without hesitation, he shoves his dick between my lips as his salty taste coats my tongue, and I swallow it down with satisfaction.

I collapse on top of Venom, and Alfa grunts, staying where he is. "Sorry, but uh... I might be here for a bit. Knotting and all that. I forgot to warn you." Alfa's voice comes out borderline pained, but I'm not bothered by what's happening. It's just a part of who he is.

"I wasn't gone that long, but it's good to see you've kept yourself occupied," Tallon says with amusement as he tucks his dick back into his pants.

Alfa snorts with laughter, still deep in my ass, and I follow him awkwardly, trying not to jostle too much. Before I know it, the whole room is alight with hysterics because, apparently, we fucked our last brain cells away. At least, it felt like it.

I smile to myself, noting how much better I've been feeling since they've accepted my needs.

Heat. What heat? The only heat I have to worry about now is the heat we work up between us that always has a happy ending.

CHAPTER 20
FAUN

WALKING DOWN THE HALL TO THE DINING ROOM, I GET THE distinct feeling that somebody's watching me and I stop, looking around for any possible danger.

"What's wrong?" Alfa asks with concern in his voice as he looks around with me, the tips of his furry ears twitching.

I frown, unsure exactly. "I don't know. I just have this weird feeling that I'm being stalked."

He laughs and puts his arm around my shoulder. "You're always being stalked here. That's nothing new, my love."

Very comforting. Thanks a lot, I think in my head, rolling my eyes at his thoughtless comment.

"What do you call a cat wearing shoes?" Styng asks, coming up beside us and nudging his head in Sabre's direction ahead of us.

I smile despite myself. "What?"

"Puss in boots." We laugh at his ridiculous joke, but when Sabre's head spins around to glare at Styng, I can't help but laugh even harder.

Alfa snorts, "What's wrong Puss, cat got your tongue?"

With lightning-fast speed, Sabre runs toward Alfa, who yelps and starts running backward, saying to Styng, "Watch her," before bolting out of the room, Sabre hot on his heels.

"You two are incorrigible." I shake my head at him, still giggling.

Hot breath ruffles the hair around my antlers, and I look back to find Ironside ridiculously close to me.

"Mayne wants you inside," he grumbles to Styng over my head. "We'll be there in a second."

Styng frowns up at him for some reason, and then looks at me for confirmation. I shoo him with a smile. I don't know why he'd be worried.

As soon as Styng leaves us, the hallway seems to be empty, but Ironside makes no move to walk inside the dining hall. I take a closer look at him and notice straight away that his pupils are enlarged, and his breathing seems to be erratic, but the strangest thing is how focused he is on me.

Shivers crawl down my spine, my heart rate picks up, and goosebumps cover my arms. "Ironside, what's wrong?" I tentatively ask, feeling a sense of danger about him, and it takes all my willpower not to step away from him.

He leans over without a sound and flops me over his shoulder, before turning and walking away from the room I was headed toward.

"What are you doing? Put me down," I squeak out, feeling super uneasy. "Where are we going?"

Someone comes jogging over to us, but I can't see who it is because I'm upside down and facing his back. I lift myself a bit and twist my body to see a smiling Alfa coming our way.

"That should hold him a while. Where are you two going?" he asks, confused, and the smile on his face drops as he sniffs the air and stiffens. "Why does Faun smell scared?"

Ironside's arm pops out and smacks Alfa straight in the face with a hard crunch, knocking him out cold. I let out a scream as he steps over his unconscious body, picking up his pace.

"What the fuck? You're scaring me." My voice comes out like a frightened squeak.

We reach Ironside's bedroom, and he closes the door behind him, locking it before answering. "I'm sorry. I need to. I'm not coping with not having touched you yet, and my beast side is taking over a bit." His normally carefree voice sounds gravelly and pained.

Understanding dawns on me, and I think about all the times my needs were screaming at me, but nobody would help, and I let my body relax.

"Okay, what do you need from me? I'm here," I tell him calmly, completely okay with taking our relationship to the next level. It's just not the way I thought it would happen.

A shuddery breath escapes him, and some tension seems to leave his shoulders. "Can I taste you?"

I have to stifle a laugh because if I've learned anything from this whole sex stuff, it's that them tasting me is *always* a good thing. "Be my guest, but you'll have to let me back up before my head explodes."

Ironside reaches up with his spare hand and rips off my underwear like it's made of paper, then lifts me up into the air.

Just as I think he's going to put me down, he opens my legs and puts one over each of his shoulders. His tongue finds my sweet spot, and he groans, the vibration rippling along my pussy, ramping up my own need.

The strength of this man astounds me as he holds me without an ounce of effort on his part. I, however, have to bend over slightly because while the ceiling is super high, it's not high enough for my antlers to not bang against it up here.

I fold myself into a comfortable position and ride out my ecstasy, twice. By the time he lays me down on the bed, stripping off his clothes, his eyes are wild with desire, and I'm shaking like a leaf from the intense pleasure.

"Turn around," Ironside orders me, and I happily comply, getting on my hands and knees. "I'm bigger than the others, by a lot, so I need you to keep still and relax. I'm going to do what I can to loosen you up a bit first."

I look over my shoulders and take in his behemoth body, and I mean, *everywhere!* "Do you want one of the others to go first?" I ask, thinking of Nanuk's approach.

Ironside growls deeply. "Mine!"

Oookay! This could be an issue later.

"Just a suggestion," I mumble.

Ironside drops to his knees behind me, pushing one digit inside my tight sheath and pumping. He works me until my breath picks up again, and he adds in a second finger, and then a third.

"Fuck. That feels so good," I groan, while his other hand focuses on my nub.

The pleasure increases, and he pushes in a fourth finger. Loud wet noises coming from me fill the room, and if I wasn't so turned on by what he's doing to me, I'd be embarrassed, but as it stands I'm about to blow.

"That's it, baby, relax into it for me," Ironside groans behind me, lust lacing every word.

Just before I cum, his hand seems to slide in further. *Oh my God, his whole hand.* He pumps me slow and deep, then lies under me to suck on my clit, and as soon as he does, I scream out, and he pulls his hand out as I gush all over his face.

After licking me all over, he gets on his knees again behind me, and I feel his dick slide inside me. I pulse around his big girth, but he just keeps pushing in until I don't think I have any room left.

"*Fuuucking helll!*" Ironside roars and starts to pump inside me. The mixture of pleasure and pain is intense, and I fear, addictive.

A sudden sting burns my ass cheek as he slaps it hard. Again and again. My pussy practically leaks from the sensation, and I cry out.

"Cum for me, Faun, one more time," his voice demands, and I almost do. Reaching under me, he pinches my clit hard. "Now!"

I scream, the pure ecstasy too intense as I pulse around him, and he follows me over the edge, calling my name as if in worship.

Slipping out of me, Ironside rolls me onto my back and looks down at me, searching my features frantically. "Are you okay? Did I hurt you? Should I call someone?"

A groggy giggle escapes me as I say, "An exorcist, because I'm sure I just had a demon in me."

My giggle intensifies like a crazy person, but I can't seem to stop. The laughter slowly turns into tears, and I start to cry, my shoulders shaking at all the intense feelings running through my body.

Ironside curses crudely and wipes the hair off my face. "I'm so sorry. I'll go and get Sabre or Mayne."

Before he can get up, I grab his wrist and pull him down to me, or more specifically, he *lets* me pull him down.

"Don't leave me. I'm just tired and overwhelmed, but I'm okay. Will you hold me for a little while?" I close my eyes and pull his heavy arm over me.

Kisses litter all over my face, tasting my tears and wiping them away. "Whatever you want, it's yours. Sleep."

CHAPTER 21
FAUN

A PAINED SQUEAL RIPS OUT OF ME INVOLUNTARILY AS I WASH MY poor, swollen lady parts. Geez, Ironside isn't for the faint of heart, but it was one hundred percent worth it.

I let the water calm my steady ache as I get used to it, and lean my head against the wall, trying to ignore the burn.

"Are you okay?" Alfa asks, knocking on my bathroom stall.

I groan at my inability to ever have a moment to myself, but answer with a grumble, "I'm alright, just a bit more tender than I'm used to."

He chuckles beyond the door and says, "Let me in, and I'll help."

"No freaking way! I'm sore as hell, and I am giving my poor bits a much-needed holiday," I snap out, making him laugh harder.

"Open the door," Alfa insists. "I'm not going to take advantage of you. I just want to help ease some of your pain. I swear, I'll keep it all above board."

I scowl at the closed door before reluctantly opening it. A very naked Alfa meets my gaze with a cheeky side smirk. I go to slam the door in his face, but his hand stops it before I can.

"I'm not getting my clothes wet. Calm down and turn around to face the wall." Alfa pushes his way into the stall, grabbing my waist and turning me around, but not before I get a load of what he's packing. Thankfully, he's not as big as some of the other guys, but in no way is Alfa small.

Letting go of me, he closes the stall, and his strong hands reach for my tense shoulders, kneading them and rolling his thumbs in a way that has me moaning and resting my head on the white-tiled wall.

Alfa growls low behind me. "You're not making it easy for me, my love. Moan like that again, and your sexy butt is going to need to be cleaned again."

I try to keep my lips closed and my sounds to a minimum as he massages down my back deeply and thoroughly, pushing his fingers into my tired muscles, his thumbs circling my lower back above the curve of my ass like a pro.

My body becomes so relaxed that I almost start to drool on the wall, my face now pushed into it as I relax further.

"Is that good? Do your muscles feel a bit better?" he asks me, leaning in so close that his lips brush against the pointed tip of my sensitive ears.

All I can do is moan in affirmation because my brain has left the building at this point, and all that's left of me is a gooey pile of relaxation.

Alfa laughs quietly and turns off the water. I attempt a growl of discontent at him stopping, but I just don't have the energy to back it up.

"Come on, it's time to get out and face the day."

"Nope," I complain. "I'm going back to bed now."

I hear Alfa open the door before I'm spun around and flung over his shoulder, with my wet, vulnerable ass up in the air.

Slap.

I'm jolted awake more by a stinging handprint growing on my butt cheek. "Hey!" Another one lands on the other, and his sharp teeth carefully nip at my hip. I'm so surprised that Alfa would spank me; I'd expect it from some of the other guys, but my Alfa is usually so sweet. Not that I'm complaining.

Alfa slides me down the front of his body and against his hard erection, and it momentarily catches my attention as I look down at it.

"Don't look at him like that. I'm trying to keep him in line as it is." Alfa grabs my shoulders and steps back, putting more distance between us. "Dry yourself and get dressed. I'm taking you to breakfast."

My thighs rub together at the incredible sight of Alfa wet and hard for me, but the friction makes me wince, quickly reminding me why I said no to begin with.

With a conceding sigh, I turn from him and grab my towel. By the time I've dried myself, Alfa is already dressed. Even though, by the wet patches on his clothes, his skin was still moist.

"You could have used my towel." I frown at him.

With a smile, he passes me my simple flowy green dress. "What I really needed was to get my dick confined as soon as possible. I'm fine this way. It's just a bit of water. I'll dry off in no time."

I pull my dress over myself with a small smile, deciding to forgo my underwear and bra today. My lady lips need the cool air and honestly, it'll hurt way too much having the material on it.

Alfa quirks one brow but doesn't object as he gathers the rest of my belongings, before entwining the fingers of his spare hand with mine. "Come on, my love. Let's go eat."

I BITE into my flavorful lasagna, and Mayne winks at me. There's something really nice about being served by all these big men. Every day I come to the dining hall, I have my favorite foods and an apple juice waiting for me.

"Faun needs a break from all the dick, so keep it in your pants, guys," Alfa suddenly says, way too freaking loud, and I choke on my mouthful.

Ironside growls low at Alfa as the others stare at me, their food frozen halfway to their mouths.

"Here." Nanuk passes me my juice while rubbing my back as I splutter and cough in the most unladylike manner ever.

My cheeks turn pink, and with wide eyes, I look at Alfa, who just shrugs in response. "It's true."

I get control of myself and grumble quietly, "Did you have to tell the whole room?" Looking around, I see way too many people staring and laughing. *Just kill me now.*

"Did I hurt you?" Ironside asks, his normally dark gray skin turning pale with concern.

Shaking my head, I reach over and touch his hand. "It's not like that."

"You've had a lot of dicks this week, so I'm not surprised," Steve remarks matter-of-factly while chewing on his burger, and my ears pick up multiple giggles around the room on my behalf. "Let us know when you're ready to go again. I'm sure that everyone wants a go, and I'm definitely gonna need to get in between your legs again soon. After all, once you go doe, there's nowhere else to go."

Sabre whacks the back of his head hard enough that his forehead smacks against his saucy plate.

"What the fuck, bro?" Steve shouts, wiping tomato sauce off his nose and forehead. "That hurt!"

"You're such an idiot. I swear to God, I don't know how you've survived this long," Sabre grumbles.

Styng leans in conspiratorially and whispers just for our table to hear, "I say we vote him off the island."

Laughter bubbles from my mouth at the double reference to our future and one of the shows Styng and I always watch together. The table joins in, with a clueless and confused-looking Steve still wiping condiments off his face, which only makes me laugh harder.

We eat jovially after that, and the males of my heart pass me around for cuddles as I sit on their laps, oblivious to the rest of the room because fuck them. I don't care about their opinions, we're happy and that's all that matters.

Little did I know that it was just the start of some very bizarre mating rituals.

OVER THE NEXT WEEK, the strangest things started happening. I keep finding large piles of shit outside my door, which I eventually learn is Ironside's way of claiming me as his. *Ew!* There's also the fact that he keeps randomly attacking or hitting other males in my vicinity, including from our pack.

Tallon keeps shoving food in my mouth every time I am near him, and at this rate, I'm going to be as big as a house by the time I get out of here. He also keeps taking me back to his room to hang out, which by itself isn't weird, but his entire room is covered with the stolen pillows and blankets from other Broken in the facility. Everyone is super pissed off, but not enough to start a fight with our pack.

Styng has been waving his tail at me every chance he gets, and randomly starts dancing at me like some kind of one-man entertainment crew. His face is so freaking serious, too, that it's hard for me to keep a straight face. It's just so funny.

Luckily, Alfa's only major change in behavior is just him being overly affectionate. He's either playing with my hair, rubbing my back, or, in the most intense cases, licking my cheek and neck. If it was anyone else, it would be cringe-worthy, but I don't mind so much when Alfa does it.

Nanuk is all about tracking me. Everywhere I go, I can turn to find him watching me and every move I make. I don't feel threatened at all. It's actually kind of cute. It's like he's always waiting for me to call him over or something. Whenever we're close enough to touch, he drops his head and starts nuzzling into my chest, but for some reason, it doesn't feel sexual—it's more of an affectionate act.

It's been particularly peculiar watching Mayne and Sabre embrace their feline sides so deeply. The two normally staunch, serious males have been reduced to purring kitties. Between the two of them rolling all over my bed, rubbing up against my furniture, and stroking me constantly while they purr, it's taken all of my self-control not to burst out laughing at them both. Especially when they're doing it at the same time, and they end up hissing and growling at each other.

Steve, by far, has been the most hilarious to watch as he prances around without a shirt to show off his chest, a wide grin plastered on his face. Anyone would think he's a Broken peacock. His loud, obnoxious grunting can be heard right down the hall, and the more people surrounding us, the more posturing and racket making he does, even snapping his teeth at people as they walk by.

Venom and I sit quietly next to each other in the dining hall as we watch the latest public mating display that the others are putting on en masse. A snicker escapes his amused face, and I raise an eyebrow at him.

"What?" he asks, feigning innocence, and I merely scoff in response. "Oh, come now, you can't tell me you don't find their outrageous performance amusing?"

Rolling my lips in, I squeeze them together tightly to keep in the laugh bubbling up inside me, wanting to escape. "I don't know what you're talking about." The last thing I want to do is belittle their acts of affection for me. "Besides, I haven't seen you dance, growl, or nest for me yet. Where's your show of devotion, buddy?"

Of course. I'm totally kidding, but I am a little curious as to why Venom is the same as he's always been, besides sneaking in a kiss here and there.

He chuffs and kisses the back of my hand. "Don't you know, precious? My act of love is to die for you, and I'd do it in a heartbeat if it meant to make you happy or safe."

My heart stutters at his declaration, and I suck in a breath. "No. If you want to show me that you love me, then I demand you live." My voice doesn't come out as strong as I'd like because the idea of losing any of my pack is too much to even contemplate.

Venom puts his arm around my shoulder and pulls me into his hard, cool body. "As you wish, but if you change your mind, you can eat me anytime." His wink and unusually cheeky grin give away his innuendo, and it blows away the shadows my thoughts were conjuring.

"How does it feel, doe?" Sylva chuckles, sliding up behind us, and I feel Venom tense beside me.

My heartbeat skyrockets even though I know that Venom will protect me, but the memories of my past, of Sylva restraining me as my friends die right in front of my eyes, will haunt me forever. His very voice is enough to make me tremble, and the sick bastard loves it.

I straighten my spine and try to hide my fear, undoubtedly failing at it. "How does what feel?"

Adda hisses as she snickers, "Finally being hunted by your pack like the prey that you are?" Her cruel smile grows creepily as she adds, "When they've taken all they want from your body, you'll be nothing but food. I do hope you'll share Venom. I bet Faun will be sssucculent."

The two of them laugh darkly and Venom pulls me behind his back at the same time that the rest of my men take notice and surround them.

Sylva snorts in amusement. "Don't worry. We're leaving. See you soon, doe."

Sylva turns and pushes in between Nanuk and Sabre as they growl fiercely, barely holding themselves back. Adda's tongue flicks against my earlobe and I flinch, realizing my mistake at focusing on Sylva.

"I promissse, my pathetic little friend, that your time isss almossst up. One way or another, I will end you," Adda hisses into my ear before slithering away, the confidence in her words making me shudder.

CHAPTER 22
MAYNE

THE NEED TO CLAIM FAUN IS GETTING OUT OF CONTROL. THE Beast part of me roaring inside at the knowledge that other males have been inside her while I've been patiently waiting.

I growl under my breath as I wash my face, needing to clear my head a bit more before I join the others in the game room. The cold liquid covers my skin and abundance of hair as I practically dive underneath the faucet of the sink.

"What's crawled up your ass?" Steve asks in greeting as he enters the shared bathroom.

Standing back up, I wipe a hand over my wet hair, sticking it back in a half-assed attempt to get it under control, but of course, it just pops back out in the wild way that it does.

"That fucking prick, Sylva," I say, in way of an explanation, because it's a half-truth. "I can feel that he's working up to something with the way his eyes have been following Faun around the room lately."

Steve walks straight to the urinal and starts relieving himself. "It's not him you need to worry about, I don't reckon. Adda has noticed too, and you know she's a green-eyed bitch when it comes to him. If anyone's going to attack Faun, it'll be her, just for getting Sylva's attention."

Sometimes I forget how smart Steve actually is. He always acts like a total dumbass, but there's so much more to him than that... I need to give him more credit than I do.

"I hadn't noticed it, to be honest," I admit as he joins me at the sink, washing his hands. "I've been too focused on that stupid ape. Good catch, my brother. I'll make sure I pay more attention in the future."

With a small smile between us, we walk out together in companionable silence before I ask, "Tell me it's worth the wait?" I can't help it, it just slips out.

Steve's understanding gaze catches me, and I'm grateful that I don't need to clarify my envy. "Definitely."

I sigh and clap his shoulder before we enter the game room. "I thought so." I wish it made me feel better, but it really doesn't.

The scene before me has me stopping in my tracks, eyes wide with a snarl threatening to escape. Six different males from various packs are flouncing around Faun, posturing themselves while trying to get her attention.

"What the fuck?" Steve asks under his breath.

The rest of our pack practically has her squished in between them, with murder in their eyes. Ironside thrusts forward and slams his Goliath fist into a Broken tiger's face when he steps too close to them, ramping up his purring. The cracking of his nose is so loud I almost flinch.

It doesn't deter the other males, though, as a Broken wolf brazenly pulls his dick out and goes to pee on the floor, hoping to mark the area with his scent. Before he gets more than a couple of drips out, Styng cuts the damn thing right off with his pincer.

A piercing scream from the now-eunuch fills the room, snapping me out of my shock.

Running forward, I take the nearest male by the neck and roar in fury as I throw him across the room. It seems to stir everyone else into a frenzy as we all start attacking the remaining males, bloodthirsty and furious that they would even attempt to sway our female away.

Bloodlust fills me as I smash in the face of a male below me. I don't even know who or what he is at this point, because all I see is rage.

Animalistic sounds fill my thrumming ears, and yet somehow a small gasp of fear trickles through the clamoring noises and pierces my heart.

My head snaps up in Faun's direction through the fray, and I freeze as Sylva leans in close, with only Tallon's smaller body in between the two.

Focusing on my new target, I storm across the room, pushing aside anyone stupid enough to be in my way.

"I think it's time you got shown how a *real* male fucks, don't you?" Sylva asks Faun, ignoring Tallon completely as if he's not there at all.

The male in question moves to cover her behind him and snarls out, "Back off shit for brains. You're not wanted here."

Sylva moves quickly, hitting Tallon so hard that he careens across the room as if he were a mere nuisance. He grabs a hold of Faun's arm roughly, dragging her into his big body as a terrified squeal comes out of her. "You're coming with me." Sylva adjusts his cock, and I go mad with fury.

"Get. Your. Fucking. Hand. Off. Her. Now!" I growl so loud that most of the males around us cease fighting and stare in awe.

My claws pop out, and I strike along his back. Deep, thick lines appear, before trickling with blood, and he howls in pain, dropping his grasp on my female and turning to me, teeth clenched in pain and eyes narrowed in outrage.

"Get her out of here!" I yell out as Sylva dives for me, knowing one of my pack will comply.

I dodge his attack and claw at his back once more, striking just as deep as before. "You're no match for me, monkey. Fuck off, with your tail between your legs where it belongs, and if you *ever* touch my female again, I will gut you and hang you by your entrails as a warning to the rest of these baboons."

With a snarl, Sylva leaps for me again, but this time I aim for his ugly-ass face, ripping ribbons through his cheeks until his teeth are visible through the parted flesh, before a river of blood coats him.

His large hands grab at the grotesquely torn features on the left side of his face, eyes wide with shock, before stepping back with a pained growl.

"We're not done," Sylva snarls as he retreats, the rest of the males hot on his heels after my pack's display of violent rebuke.

As soon as they're gone, my eyes flick around with worry, trying to find Faun, but Alfa steps forward with his hands raised. "Tallon and Styng took her back to her room like you said."

My body instantly sags in relief, but not enough for me to relax—I need to see she's okay with my own eyes. "I'll take care of her, go clean up," I demand, noticing that they're as bloody with others' pain as I am.

I'm more than aware that I should wash off before I go and see her, but my beast riles inside me, unable to calm until I have Faun by my side, safe and unharmed. I stride down the hall with undoubtedly wild eyes, looking like someone who just stepped out of a horror film. I couldn't give two shits what others think of me, though, and if it helps to remind them why I'm not to be fucked with, then even better.

I fling Faun's door open, stepping inside and pointing to it. "Get the fuck out," I growl at Tallon and Styng, unable to do civility right now.

"Are you sure about that?" Styng asks warily, and my eyes trail over him, darkening.

"Are you challenging me?" I growl, ready to fight for the right to be with my female if I'm pushed.

Styng shakes his head nervously, flicking his gaze between Tallon and me. "No. Of course not, but I don't want you to hurt her. You need to calm down." His voice is soft and more than a bit concerned, and I try desperately to focus on that as I close my eyes and take a deep breath, relaxing my shoulders and telling myself that everything is okay.

"I'm calm, and would never hurt her, I just need to be alone," I speak every word as softly as I can muster, which frankly isn't very soft, but that's not who I am on the best of days.

I open my eyes and land them on the small figure behind Styng, looking up at me with her soft gaze, completely unafraid of me, even though I must look frightful.

Tallon steps forward and grabs Styng's arm. "Come on, they'll be fine." His faith in all of us is unmeasured, and I've never been more grateful for it.

I nod in thanks, never taking my eyes off the most beautiful, bewitching creature I've ever known, and wait for them to leave, relaxing even more when the door clicks closed behind me.

"I need to hold you, beautiful," I admit, letting myself be vulnerable for the first time in my life. "I need to feel that you're alright."

Faun's concerned gaze travels down my body, and she steps forward. "Are you hurt? You're all bloody," she asks, her worry for me evident, and it warms my heart even further.

"It's not my blood," I say before thinking, cringing at what a monster I must seem to her right now.

Faun approaches me carefully, reaching up and trailing her delicate fingers over my heavily bearded cheek. "Did you kill him?"

"Not yet, but he's certainly not as pretty as he used to think he was," I grunt out, trying not to pounce on her as her soft touch trails my scorching skin. "Do you want me to? Because I will."

My heart rate picks up as she gets on her tiptoes, her sweet lips only inches from mine. "You're my hero, you know that? What I really want is for you to kiss me." Her breathy voice makes me shudder.

"If I taste you now, I won't be able to stop; and I won't be able to take you the way you deserve," I tell her honestly, my hands squeezing into fists by my side in an attempt to keep control of myself.

Without an ounce of hesitation, Faun's arms wrap around my neck, and she crashes her lips onto mine, her tongue instantly demanding entry.

All of my resolve shatters into a million pieces as I return her hungry kiss with my own, my bloodied hands gripping her ass and lifting her into my embrace.

Faun's long legs wrap around my hips and I turn, slamming her body against the door and grinding my throbbing dick against her core. With a growl, I lift one hand, ripping her shirt open in the front, needing to see her golden flesh.

Her perky breasts bounce as I free them, tearing her bra in the center, revealing tasty pebbled nipples begging for me to feast on.

A growl rips from my throat, and I lift her higher as I wrap my lips around the juicy peaks. Her needy moans spur me on, and I drop to my knees, placing one of her legs over my shoulder. I use my extended claws to split the seam of her leggings open, delighted to find her bare pussy gleaming at me. *No panties, I like it.*

My mouth dives onto her, and I taste her sweet saltiness with a groan. There's no way I can hold off anymore, even though I know I'm supposed to make this about her.

I delve my tongue into her tight confines and nuzzle into her core, letting her juices coat my face with a purr that makes her tremble and moan.

Unable to fight my instincts anymore, I stand back up, wrapping her legs around me again. Lining myself up, I thrust into her straight away, hard. Probably too hard, but I can't stop as I pound deep inside her again and again. My mind is relieved as she grasps onto me, crying out in pleasure and not pain because I couldn't bear it if I hurt her.

I squeeze her tight ass, my claws digging in as I try to get closer to her, needing more. "Fuck," I growl deeply, pulling out and turning her around on her feet, slamming her against the door, pulling her hips back, and entering her from behind with a hard thrust.

Faun cries out into the wooden door, her scream slightly muffled. "More," she moans, and I go wild, rocking into her harder and harder before leaning in and biting her shoulder to keep her in place.

Take it all!

Her moans of encouragement undo me, and I cum deep inside her, letting her flesh go with my mouth and growling low before going slack.

I pant against the back of her head and push her body flush against the wooden surface, wanting to cover her completely. The rise and fall of her shoulders as she breathes calm my rapid heartbeat, and I feel my body completely relaxing for the first time since I can remember... But that's when I realize that my claws are embedded into her hips.

Retracting them as quickly as I can, I retreat from her with a curse, the scent of her blood in the air. *No. No. No. What have I done?*

Faun turns and leans against the door with a strange euphoric look that doesn't make any sense. What kind of monster am I that I could injure this perfect female?

"I'm so sorry, beautiful." My broken voice falters as horror fills me at what I've done.

Faun frowns and tilts her head in confusion. "What for?" She walks toward me, her clothes torn and bloody with both her and Sylva's blood, and I recoil, stepping back. "What's wrong, Mayne? Did I do something?"

The concern in her voice squeezes my heart even more. "I didn't mean to hurt you. It shouldn't have been like that. I should have left. I knew I'd hurt you. I just *knew* it." My gaze drops to the floor in regret, unworthy to even be in her presence.

What kind of leader am I if I hurt the person I love the most in this world? After all these years of pining for Faun, I had to ruin it by being the monster I can never hide from.

As I wallow in my self-pity, Faun comes to me and places her hand over my heart. "It was perfect, and I wouldn't change a thing, so don't ruin this moment by being your pigheaded, somber self. I love you and I love how hard and deep you took me. It's exactly what I needed today, and you'd better do it again in the future, too." Her tone is clear and honest, which surprises me.

I look into her eyes and find only sincerity, understanding, and love. I let my head lean against hers and close my eyes, astounded by how perfect she is for me, and the depths of my devotion to her. I would set fire to the sea if it meant she'd be happy.

"I really didn't hurt you?" I ask, needing to hear it one more time.

Faun tugs on my beard and replies, "Oh, you hurt me alright, and it was hot as all hell. Next time you bite me like that, pull my hair as well."

A laugh snorts out of me unexpectedly. *This female is something else.*

CHAPTER 23
FAUN

"It's official: I love my life," I say with a yawn as I stretch across the couch, my head in Styng's lap.

He looks down at me with an abundance of love in his eyes, and for a moment, I get lost in the dark depths. That is until his tail rises over his head and starts dancing to the cha-cha.

I stifle a laugh and stroke his soft jaw. "I love you, you know that, right?" Having so many men in my life, I always want to make it a priority to tell them all how much they mean to me. I would hate for any of them to not realize how important they are in my heart.

"I know. Hey, did you know that kangaroos can jump higher than the Empire State Building?" Styng asks me, as random as ever.

I squint my eyes at him. "I highly doubt that." How the heck would that work?

"No, it's true," he exclaims with rounded eyes. "Buildings can't jump."

"Oh my God." I roll my eyes and turn back to the TV as he chuckles. "You're ridiculous. This is why I can never take you seriously."

Styng kisses my cheek and strokes my antlers and hair, paying attention to the show again. "You know you love it."

I let my eyes close, enjoying the feeling of him touching me so gently. "That feels really nice," I moan into his lap, and I feel his dick twitch next to my face.

The cheeky side of me wakes up and pays attention, and I rub my face in his lap some more with another moan. Styng stops moving his hand and hardens more beneath me.

I turn around on the seat until I'm facing him instead of the TV, giving him my best come-hither eyes as I rub my cheek along the hard bulge building in his pants.

"What are you doing?" Styng practically whispers, clearly affected by my intimate caress.

I sit up and straddle his lap. "What aren't you doing?" I ask, grinding myself on his lap, wanting to get closer to him than I've had a chance to up until now.

Styng, clearly not wanting to waste this opportunity either, leans into me with a smile, kissing my lips with a soft caress and wrapping his arms around me, his large pincer pulling me in closer.

I enjoy the feeling of our lips tenderly brushing against each other, neither of us in a hurry. We taste and nip with adoration and trust, while our hands stroke and touch as if to cement this moment into our memories forever.

We kiss like that for what feels like an eternity, before being abruptly interrupted when the door of the room swings open and slams closed. An irritated, grumbling Sabre stalks in and plops down beside us on the couch, his arms crossed and sharp teeth more prominent than usual with his sneer of distaste.

"What crawled up your butt and died?" Styng asks him, while still stroking my back lovingly.

Sabre looks over as if just realizing we are there, and takes in our position with a raised brow. "Ah, sorry, did I interrupt something?" he asks, rubbing the back of his neck uncomfortably.

"It's fine. What's wrong?" I ask, worried about him because he doesn't often get flustered.

Sabre shakes his head, scowling. "Fucking Ironside, that's what's wrong. Who in their right mind thinks it's acceptable to take a giant shit in the middle of the hallway? I went to check on you and almost fell in it. I get that he's marking his territory and all that crap, but for fuck's sake, can't he just write 'mine' on your door instead? It's a fuck load more sanitary."

Laughter bubbles out of me and Styng at the same time, earning a deeper scowl from my grumpy male, and it only makes me laugh harder.

"It's not funny, it's disgusting," Sabre grumbles unhappily.

I lean over. "Come here and give me a kiss," I tell him, knowing it'll change his mood, and I smile brightly as his eyes light up with interest.

Scooching over, he grabs my jaw and kisses me deeply. Styng clears his throat, making me break the kiss with a giggle.

"Are you feeling left out?" I ask sweetly.

Styng grinds my hips against his hard cock. "I hate to sound like I'm complaining, but I'm the only one that hasn't had you all the way yet, and I'm feeling a little needy."

I scowl and realize that he's right, and there's no way that I'm not rectifying that right this very minute. I slide off his lap and get to my knees, parting his legs, so I can move between them. Looking up at him, I get a thrill out of watching his hard, nervous swallow as I peel down the zipper of his pants. I reach in and pull out his smooth, velvety dick that's so hard I wonder if it hurts.

I ignore the groan of need that comes from Sabre, as I bend forward with my eyes still locked on Styng's and take the tip of his cock into my mouth, rolling my tongue around it, enjoying his salty taste.

Styng's mouth drops open with a whoosh of air and his head lolls back, losing our connection, and I focus on sucking him down as deep as I can into my mouth, letting the tip push into my throat enough that I gag on him slightly.

I bob up and down as Styng's breathing becomes more erratic, and he curses quietly at the intense feeling.

"I want some," Sabre complains, and I let Styng's dick come out of my mouth with an audible pop. I look over at Sabre, who is holding onto his own with a tight squeeze.

It's obvious that if I keep going as I am, Styng's going to combust before I get to fuck him. I sit back and tell him to take off his pants, as I pull my own down and kick them off, and then move to kneel in front of Sabre.

He strokes his dick up and down slowly, looking at me with hooded eyes and a fuck load of lust.

"Now what?" Styng asks, and Sabre scoffs loudly.

"Say Grace and fuck Faun until she gags on me. What else, numbnuts?" Sabre snarks at him, moving to the edge of the seat, and I suck him down with one big gulp. "Fuuuck!"

I feel Styng grab my hips and guide his thankfully normal-sized cock to my wet entrance, sliding it up and down my slick folds before pushing inside me smoothly, my body sucking him in like its favorite candy, while Sabre grabs my antlers to pull my mouth down harder onto his cock.

"You're so fucking good at that," he moans, and the three of us get into a pounding rhythm that has me both choking and moaning.

Sabre's balls tighten, and I feel the moment before he lets go. Sucking him all the way down my throat, he climaxes with a roar, and Styng picks up his pace, grabbing one hip roughly while thrusting as deep and hard as he can. My pleasure skyrockets and as soon as I cum, he follows me, falling over my back with a groan and a curse.

A smile lines my lips, as I lay with my eyes closed in Sabre's lap with Styng resting on me. I live for moments like these lately, when we're all as vulnerable and sated as each other. There's something so intimate about it.

I open my eyes to stare directly into Venom's as he cums silently in his hand. And holy shit, if that doesn't turn me on again. I wink at him, and he blows me a kiss.

"Enjoy the show?" I ask, making the other two jolt with surprise as they look over at the smiling assassin in the shadows.

Tucking his dick away, he chuckles. "Best show I've seen in ages."

"Seriously Venom?" Styng groans, standing back up behind me and pulling his pants back on. "At least let us know you're here next time."

Hopefully, that means he can watch more. I never knew I'd like that, but the idea of him cumming just from watching does all sorts of forbidden things to me.

CHAPTER 24

FAUN

Humming happily to myself, I smooth the oil over my antlers, making sure not to miss a spot. A girl has to take care of her best attributes, after all.

My life has changed so significantly over the last few months, and as I look in the mirror, it's hard to recognize the past me in the reflection. The me that didn't know I had an expiration date and didn't know what it was to feel the touch of a man in the way I do now, let alone nine of them. I feel simultaneously safer and more fragile.

I tilt my head, parting the side of my hair as I begin to braid my long blond locks, still humming the same cheerful tune. Even though I know I'm meant to be more scared than I am about being exterminated, I can't help but hold on to my hope that everything will work out; and that one day I will feel freedom caress my cheeks as I sit on our island, soaking in the rays of the sun.

My nose twitches as I scent dirty leather, and I freeze, my heart missing a beat. *Sylva.* I focus on my hearing, turning my ears slightly, but it's too late. They're here.

I suck in a deep breath slowly, tying the end of my braid and turning around, not at all surprised to find Sylva, Fang, and King leaning against the back wall of the girls' locker room as if they don't have a care in the world.

"What do you want?" I speak in a sharp, clipped tone, attempting to cover up the unavoidable fear trickling down my spine. *Why did I come in here alone? Stupid.*

Sylva pushes off the wall and lumbers over to me as the other two snicker like weasels. "I see you're feeling brave today, doe. Good thing too. You're going to need all the fire you've got to keep up with me."

Fuck, no! "Styng is right outside," I threaten. "You don't have a chance to hurt me." *God, I hope that's true.*

Sylva's two lackeys join him as he stands just out of arm's reach of me, his large, apelike body taking up way too much space for my comfort.

"You know you want it. We've been scenting desperation from you for weeks now, and I think it's only charitable of me to help you out," Sylva insists, sneering at me and licking his lips. "I know exactly how to make you scream. I might even let you have a pleasurable one too."

Faster than I can track, Fang slips around me and grabs me from behind, pulling my hands behind my back with his python grip. I try to writhe away from him, but I don't budge. Terror fills me and Sylva grips my hips tightly, moving in so close that he pins me between their bodies, making it hard to breathe.

"Let me go!" I scream, flinging my head from side to side, trying to skewer them with my antlers, but I can't get the right angle. "Help!" I yell as loud as I can, praying to God that Styng or one of the others can hear me.

Sylva's disgusting lips land on mine and I whack my head forward, slamming my head into his nose with a crack.

With a bellow of rage and pain, he moves back and slaps me hard across my face, my head whipping to the side with the impact, a tinge of blood on my tongue.

Before I can react further, Sylva gets ripped from my body by a furious Ironside, who then throws him to the ground, pummeling his gigantic fists into Sylva's face.

Fang changes his grip, wrapping his arms around me and squeezing. Instantly I know I'm in grave danger because he is known for killing his enemies through constriction.

Fang's chilling chuckle tickles my ear. "Night, night, little prey." His long, forked tongue licks my lobe, and I shudder as I try to catch my fading breath.

"Let her go, Fang," Mayne demands with a furious roar, an equally tumultuous Sabre at his side. They know that he can snap me like a twig if they even try to interfere, and are probably hoping they can talk him down.

Unfortunately, he only tightens his grip, and I fear my death is imminent as my ribs threaten to crack.

A loud gasp from the male behind me takes me by surprise, and his grip loosens straight away. The sudden flow of oxygen and blood makes me light-headed, and I instantly start to fall.

Styng catches me before I can and lifts me into his arms, cradling me like an adored bride. "I'm so sorry that I didn't come sooner." His normally jovial voice cracks with heavy emotion, and I snuggle my head into his chest as I catch my breath, grateful that he found me at all.

I look over to see Mayne and Sabre pulling Ironside off a bloodied and badly beaten Sylva, still clearly alive but a lot worse for wear. His buddy King helps get him to his feet, pulling him away from my packmates, his own face cracked and swollen, showing off his newly acquired injuries that I missed out on seeing him get.

They back out of the room, Sylva barely able to walk. Ironside huffs and pants angrily, staring after them as if letting them leave is the hardest thing he's ever done, vengeance and bloodlust in his eyes.

"What about Fang?" I croak out to Styng, and his arms stiffen around me.

"He won't be bothering you again. I made sure of that." Styng's voice is dark and unrecognizable.

I turn my head to peer around him, spotting Fang's limp body on the floor, his lifeless eyes staring off into the distance. Styng's poison is just as potent as Venom's, but unlike Venom, Styng has never wanted or needed to use his, and I have no doubt that this will haunt his dreams even though he did it for me.

I nuzzle into him. "Oh, Styng. I'm sorry you had to do that." My beautiful man has always lived in his happy place, wanting to bring joy to everyone around him. To know that he went against his values and killed a person for me breaks my heart.

"I would do it a thousand times over if it meant saving you. Never be sorry about that." He holds me close to him, rubbing his cheek against mine lovingly.

A large arm encircles my waist and rips me from Styng's grasp. I'm firmly yanked into Ironside's chest, the vibration of his low growl giving away his foul mood.

Without a word, he storms past Mayne and Sabre, stalking heavily down the hall and into my room, not even bothering to close my door as he lays me down and half covers my body with his.

Ironside's massive size is cumbersome and suffocating, but try as I may to budge him off me, he doesn't move an inch, only growling instead.

"Ironside, you've gotta let Faun up, you're gonna crush her," Styng warns him, coming up to the side of my bed.

The low growling intensifies the closer Styng gets, and Mayne grabs his arm and tells him to stop, seeing the clear threat and thankfully taking it seriously. "Just give him some space until he calms down."

Feeling his possessive need, I decide to relax into this because he's not going anywhere, anytime soon. I stroke my fingers softly up and down his arm and say quietly, "Hey big guy, how about you give my lungs a little extra air, okay? You don't have to leave. Just scooch over a bit."

With a grunt of affirmation, he lifts some of his heavy weight off my chest and slides to the side, making me much more comfortable. I thank him and keep stroking his tough skin, feeling his body begin to relax under my caress.

Tallon's voice catches my attention, and I look over to him and all the others that have gathered at the door to see what's happening. "We need to move away and give Ironside some space. I'd put money on him needing to claim her again after everything that happened."

"He's not the only one," Sabre grumbles, crossing his arms over his chest petulantly.

Mayne agrees with Tallon though, and ushers everyone out except for him and Sabre, closing themselves inside the room with us.

"Listen here, Ironside. We're not leaving, to make sure that Faun's safe, but just pretend like we're not here. We will stay sitting against the door and won't approach the bed unless she's in danger. Grunt if you understand," Mayne explains slowly as he and Sabre slide down the door, sitting down with their arms perched on their knees.

Ironside grunts in response while sliding his hand under my shirt and up my stomach to rest over my heart.

"I need to be close to you." His gravelly voice right next to the tip of my ear makes it twitch.

Understanding dawns on me and I say softly, squeezing his shoulder, "Let me take my clothes off, and we can snuggle. I'm all yours for the rest of the day."

Reluctantly, Ironside rolls off me and stands beside the bed, instantly pulling his shirt over his head and dropping his pants to the floor, his large body fully bared to me, and I'm surprised to note that he doesn't seem to be aroused in the slightest.

I sit up and undress completely, leaving nothing on that could be a barrier between us. Sabre sucks in a breath from the doorway, but I remain focused on Ironside and his needs as his eyes feast on my body, filled with adoration instead of desire.

Ironside pulls back the blankets of my bed and wiggles his way down the bed until he's comfortable, reaching his hand out for me to join him. I hop in beside him and snuggle close to his leathery body, resting my cheek on his huge bicep so that my antlers don't get in the way.

"Why don't you stay with me tonight?" I ask, looking at his bloodied fists and wishing I wasn't the cause of so much discourse.

Regardless of the fact that I've never actually done anything to deserve the way people outside my pack treat me, I can't help but feel guilty about a life being taken today. It could have been so different if they hadn't held such unnecessary contempt for me.

"Get out of your own head, Faun," Ironside grumbles deeply. "I know that look, and I won't have it. Now close your eyes and rest. It'll make my inner beast calm down more."

Surprisingly, I do feel exhausted after everything that happened today. The adrenaline dump, as usual, makes me lethargic and ready for sleep.

Closing my eyes, I smile softly as he leans closer and kisses me tenderly on the tip of my nose. For such a big beefy guy, Ironside can be so incredibly gentle when the mood strikes, or maybe it's just for me. It's hard to tell.

As I start to drift off, I hear Mayne whisper to Ironside, "Sleep well, my brother. She's safe, and we won't be far." The light switches off, and he and Sabre exit the room, closing the door behind them and leaving silence reigning in the dark. The only sound is our combined breath and the beating of our steady heartbeats.

CHAPTER 25
ALFA

Hearing about how close Faun came to death today freaks me the hell out. We do such a great job of keeping her safe usually, considering how many people here want to see her dead just because she's prey, but in just one moment of weakness she gets snatched up. We can't let that happen again.

"I don't even know whose turn it was to watch her," Nanuk states, picking at his dinner.

The two of us are the only ones still left in the dining hall because everyone else lost their appetite over Sylva's stunt. He's lucky Ironside didn't kill him too.

Nanuk bites into his burger and says over his mouthful, "Serves Fang right, anyway. Stupid fuck should've expected to die over putting his dirty fucking hands on my woman."

"Our woman!" I correct sharply, feeling territorial whenever someone tries to claim her as theirs. "Besides, it should be a good reminder to everyone else here not to mess with our pack. I'm surprised they forgot after Mayne and Sabre beheaded those two bastards a few years back for pushing Faun around."

"Perhapsss, Ssstyng made a very bad missstake," Adda hisses at the nape of my neck, making my hackles rise, but before I get a chance to move, her fangs slam deep into my throat.

A burning pain rips through me and I let out an agonized howl, grabbing her head and ripping her off me. I stand up and spin around, my chair clanging to the ground, hearing the sounds of Nanuk fighting someone behind me as I face off with Adda, the filthy snake.

I step toward her but falter, and I stumble forward instead, my knees crashing to the floor in a heavy thud, the air in my lungs constricting and my eyesight flickering as my consciousness begins to fail me.

Falling face forward, I try to move my hands to stop the collision, but they're too heavy, the pain in my veins too thick, and my face smashes against the cold linoleum floor.

I barely recognize Nanuk's cries of protest as the darkness takes hold of me, my last thoughts of Faun smiling at me with her bright eyes and golden skin, loving me just the way I am.

NANUK

King's face crumbles under my fist when I ram it home again. The stupid fool choosing to keep fighting us, even after his ass whooping earlier.

With triumph, I watch his body keel over as he writhes in agony. *Pathetic!* I turn to Alfa to joke about how easy it is to take down a joker named King when his knees fall to the ground, his body swaying precariously as Adda sneers down at him with callous fascination, and all at once, realization hits.

That bitch!

I roar with a fury so loud that it reverberates off the walls and jump clear over the table, landing just in time for Alfa to crumble at my feet, the life in his body fighting for survival.

Torn whether to attack Adda for doing this to him or to help my brother, she makes the choice for me, sprinting from the room, leaving behind her malicious laughter.

"Alfa," I cry out, my heart in my throat. "Please wake up."

My fingers search his throat, beside two puncture marks where Adda clearly bit him, and find only a slow, unsteady beat.

I look up and see the guards on duty just leaning against the wall, watching with mild interest as my friend dies on the floor. "Help him!" I demand with a guttural growl.

Instead of heeding my call, they look at each other and laugh. Fucking laugh. I jump to my feet and run at them full speed, my claws extended fully and my teeth aching for their blood.

The movement spurs them into action, and they raise their guns square in my direction. "Help him or you die." I give them one last warning. "You can shoot me, but I'm taking at least one of you with me. What will it be?" I grind through clenched teeth, poised, ready to strike.

The oldest of the two rolls his eyes and pulls up his communicator. "We need a Dr. Adina to the dining room please, and some guys to carry a big fucker out of here. Looks like if he's not dead, he will be soon."

"Happy now?" the younger one asks rhetorically. "Now bugger off."

I make it back to my friend at the same time that Steve and Venom walk in to see what all the fuss is about. Their eyes lock with mine, and they see in the depths how dire the situation is.

Venom runs off to tell the others, while Steve joins me on Alfa's other side, unshed tears rimming his wide eyes. "Adda?" he asks, but all I can do is nod, my voice failing me as emotions rampage my heart. I can't lose my brother like this.

"Move," a stern female voice demands, making me look up. Hope fills me as Dr. Morigan Adina charges across the room. "Oh my God," she gasps when she sees who it is, dropping to her knees. "How did this happen?"

I explain what Adda did as quickly as I can, and she ushers

guards over to carry Alfa out, with her right on their tail shooting demands at them the whole while.

Alfa and the guards disappear through the door as a terrified Faun runs through the room sobbing loudly, and Dr. Adina turns to her, saying, "I'll do what I can." The doors close before she makes it to them, and she bangs her petite body against the solid barrier, slamming her fists against it and demanding to be let through.

The guard nearby narrows his eyes at her and reaches for his taser, so I grab her hips and haul her flailing and screaming body against mine. "It's going to be alright," I tell her with what I hope isn't a lie, and heaving cries break my heart even further than it already is.

Our pack has always been together since we were tiny boys rolling in the mud, with Faun the exception. I can't imagine my life without Alfa in it, but I have to stay strong and have hope because I can't deal with what's happening if I don't.

His heart was beating. Hold on to that. He's alive—for now.

THE NIGHT IS long and the next day is even longer as we all sit on the floor by the entrance waiting for any kind of news, but not one guard tells us anything, and we haven't seen Dr. Adina since the door closed behind her, taking Alfa's life in her hands.

"What's taking so long?" Faun asks for the hundredth time. "I don't understand. Why won't they tell us what's happening?"

Steve pulls her into his lap and wraps his arms around her. "Remember, no news is good news. Nothing travels faster than bad news, so the fact that we haven't heard anything is promising," he wisely answers, and I have to do a double-take. Who knew he had it in him? I thought the only thing Steve consisted of was dirty jokes, inappropriate comments, and a full-on sex drive.

"I know. I just hate this so much, and I'm scared," Faun croaks, her voice tired from all the crying she'd been doing.

The large steel door opens suddenly, and we all look up expectantly. Both Dr. Adinas' step through and my heart drops, making me want to vomit. It's not often that daddy dearest shows his face, so it can't be good news.

Faun sucks in a sob, and Steve hugs her sweetly.

"It's okay, my little one," Dr. Foster Adina coos to Faun, kneeling in front of her with caring eyes. "Alfa is still alive and fighting. In fact, he is doing much better than expected considering the circumstance and the amount of venom we found in his veins. The antidote is working perfectly."

We all heave a collective sigh of relief as Faun starts to cry, hiding her face in her hands and hiccuping, "Thank you so much," between each sob.

"He's not out of the woods yet." Dr. Morigan Adina adds quietly, "But by all signs, he should make a full recovery if he keeps up the fight he's been putting in."

Dr. Foster Adina strokes Faun's hair back off her face tenderly as if she were his daughter too, and Steve growls low, pulling her in tighter to his body.

"I won't hurt her Crush," he says to reassure him. "We are no threat to you or your family."

Steve immediately relaxes, a triumphant smile lighting up his face like a giant child as he looks over at us. "He called me Crush."

Faun scoffs a laugh through her tears and leans up to kiss his cheek. "He sure did, baby." She turns to Dr. Foster Adina and asks, "When can I see him?"

He looks back to his daughter, and then leans in closer to us all so that the guards can't hear him and whispers, "We can't allow you back there, but other things are progressing quickly, and we should be able to move on it, very soon."

Understanding dawns immediately, and we all nod in agreement, showing him that we comprehend his meaning, and he smiles widely in response.

"Righto, we're going to head back in and check up on our little friend. If there's any change, we'll let you know." Dr. Foster Adina stands up with a huff. "In the meantime, try to stay out of trouble, you lot."

They leave through the door, and I feel like I take the first real breath since dinner last night. The heaviness on my heart lightens now that I know Alfa's going to be okay, and that, hopefully, we'll be out of this hellhole sooner rather than later.

CHAPTER 26
FAUN

"Aahh!" I scream as I wake up from the sudden blaring of a crazy loud alarm.

Bleep. Bleep. Bleep.

The incessant racket has my heart beating out of my chest a million miles a minute, and I jump out of my skin as a large hand grabs my shoulder.

"It's just me. Calm down," Venom says in a soothing voice that's almost drowned out by the obnoxious noise surrounding us, orange lights along the wall edge flashing in the dark room, just to make the whole thing more intense.

I grind my eyes with the palm of my hand. "What on earth is going on?" I forgot for a second that I wasn't alone when I fell asleep last night, because Venom stayed over to 'distract' me from my worries about Alfa.

The pounding of feet against the polished concrete floors outside my door keeps my senses sharpened, the feeling of a threat hovering in the air, and I remember that the Ark wants to exterminate us.

"Do you think it's time? That they're finishing us?" I ask Venom nervously, and he pulls me under his arm, brushing my knotted hair off my antlers.

With a confident tone, he disagrees. "They wouldn't risk us fighting back. If they wanted us gone, I have no doubt they could do something as simple as gas us in our sleep, and we'd be none the wiser."

"Thanks," I grumble, wishing he hadn't said it like that. "That's really reassuring."

"But, just to be safe, put on some sturdy clothes and good shoes because whatever is going on, it doesn't sound good."

Agreeing with him, I jump out of bed and put on my green training gear. It fits me like a glove and gives me plenty of room to move. I quickly braid my hair back, and we head out, opening the door and peeking through the gap warily.

"Let me go first. Stay behind me," Venom orders, and I'm in no position to disagree, happily moving in behind him.

Straight away, the scent of blood carries through the air, and not a small amount of it. "I smell blood and death, Venom," I inform him, knowing his sense of smell probably won't pick it up as well, and he nods stiffly before moving out into the hallway with me close behind.

We move silently down the path, keeping close to the wall as we go. The sounds of battle and screams echo down the corridor, raising the hair on my body, my instincts screaming for me to run.

As we turn the corner, a morbid display of dead bodies litter the floor, some ripped to shreds, some in awkward positions, and some with their throats ripped out.

"We need to find the others," Venom whispers. "Let's pick up speed."

With steady, soundless footsteps, we jog carefully, my ears twitching at every sound while breathing through my mouth, the stench of death too much to deal with.

Footsteps race toward us, and we freeze, Venom changing his stance to attack when Tallon, Ironside, and Styng round the corner.

I race into Styng's open arms and ask quietly, "What's happening? Where are the others?"

Ironside answers, looking up and down the hallway on full alert. "Some of the Broken have risen up and are in full riot. They're killing anyone they can find that won't help them fight against the guards. Several of the guards on duty have been disemboweled already, including Antonio. It's only a matter of time before they come in here and execute us all."

"The others are fighting off the rebels, trying to stop them from heading down here. We need to get you somewhere safe, precious," Tallon adds, pulling on my hand to head down the way they came. "There's a supply closet down here that we should be able to jam closed from the inside. Let's go."

I can't hide and let my men fight and die and say as much, but to no avail, because they won't listen to me, practically dragging me to the room in question.

Ironside kisses my mouth hard enough to hurt, and I let him. "Please be safe," I cry out, not wanting to let him go as I cling to his wrists. "I want every one of you to come back safe to me. Do you hear me?" I demand with a broken, scared voice.

"Always." Ironside kisses me one more time and holds the door open. "In, now. Don't open the door for anyone but one of us."

Styng pulls me in tight and whispers in my ear, "What goes oo ooo oo?"

I scoff at his ridiculous timing, but my heart warms that he always wants to make me smile. "Tell me, you silly goose," I chuckle sadly.

"A cow with no lips, of course." Styng kisses the tip of my nose and smiles, "We'll be back soon, baby, keep quiet. Love you."

"Love you too."

Tallon pulls me into the dark room and closes the door, and my heart gallops as I hear my loves running away.

"I want you to keep very still till I say so, okay? Your vision isn't as good as mine in the dark, and I don't want you to get hurt." Tallon gently moves me until my back is against the wall, and he lets me go.

The sound of furniture moving around in the dark keeps me focused, and I pray that no one is around to hear it.

Tallon's hand slips into mine. "Sit down, we're safe now. There's no way they can open that door without me moving stuff. All the same, though, keep silent," he whispers, pulling me down to the ground with him, where we huddle against each other for comfort.

"Will they be alright?" I ask quietly.

"They have to be."

ALFA

A myriad of sounds break into my unconscious: alarms blaring, pounding, slamming, people talking loudly, and clamoring about.

What the hell is happening? And why do I feel so crap?

The memory of Adda biting me and pain comes roaring back, and I flinch as I open my eyes to the bright blaring lights, the sounds around me seeming louder by the second, and my senses and mind are overwhelmed.

I squint my eyes against the obnoxiously bright lights and try to sit up. My body is zapped of energy and I barely move. Looking around, I see guards running back and forth through the glass window separating me from them. The only person in the little room with me is a young male nurse, by the looks of it.

I clear my throat to get his attention, and he turns to me with wide, frightened eyes. I give him a small smile, not wanting him to view me as a threat, and ask, "What's going on?" My voice sounds cracked and unused, my mouth as dry as the desert.

"Um, uh," the nurse looks around like he's searching for an answer or a person to save him from the big bad wolf, but this wolf is handcuffed to a hospital bed and isn't that scary right now. "I'll get Dr. Adina," he finally says after stammering like a fool and scurries out of the room. I guess I'm above his pay grade.

I lay my head back and close my eyes, my stomach feeling sick and my head woozy. I feel like absolute crap, but it could be worse. I could be dead.

"Alfa, you're awake," Dr. Morigan Adina greets me with a cheerful voice, but the worry around her eyes is evident. "You had us concerned for a while there. Good thing you've got some fight in you. How are you feeling?"

She comes over and puts the back of her hand on my head before checking the machines beeping away at my side.

"I'm fine. What's going on?" I ask, more worried about the four large shoulders that just ran past the window, loaded with heavy artillery. "Should I be worried, Dr. Adina?"

With a heavy sigh, she drops her facade and says tiredly, "Please call me Morigan. It would make me feel a lot better if you did." I nod, and she goes on, kindly patting my hand. "Before I tell you what's happening, I need you to tell me the truth about how you feel, so I can help you, and we can move on from it because I need you focused."

Seeing the seriousness in her eyes, I tell her how I'm really feeling, and she gives me a shot of something that will apparently help with me feeling nauseous.

"A large portion of the Broken are rioting and have gone on a killing spree of both guard and Broken alike, and before you ask, I have no idea how anyone in your pack is doing, but I have no doubt that they aren't involved in this atrocity," Morigan tells me bluntly, pulling a small set of keys from her pocket and uncuffing me. "I don't believe these are necessary. Do you?"

I rub my sore wrists and carefully sit up in bed, having better luck this time around. "I need to get to them. I have to protect Faun." My instincts are driving me to get to her, not knowing if she's safe will drive me mad.

"I know. I feel the same. All I know is that my father is looking into it now, and he'll let us know as soon as he learns anything. For now, all we can do is wait and hope for the best."

CHAPTER 27
STYNG

WITH CONFIDENT STRIDES, WE POUND DOWN THE HALLWAY toward the sound of battle, and I try to ready myself for the conflict that I know is unavoidable.

Taking Fang's life affected me more than I'd like to admit, and it plays on my mind in a somber reel of discomfort. I logically know there was nothing else I could have done at the time, and he wasn't a good person, but it doesn't mean I have to be happy about it; and the way today's looking, he won't be the only loss weighing on my mind. Not if I want to protect myself and my pack.

I steel myself as the fight comes into view, my pack brothers in the thick of it, defending themselves the best they can, and it looks like they're doing a great job at it too, by the bodies already littered at their feet.

Just as Mayne and Sabre spot me and Venom, a male Broken shark comes running at me from the side, but before he catches a hold of me, Ironside tackles him to the ground with his formidable size and starts to pummel his face into the ground without mercy, blood pooling quickly at his knees as Ironside straddles the attacker's body.

"Where is she?" Mayne booms at us, and I turn to find him

distracted from the fight and staring with concern behind me. "Where. Is. Faun?"

Sabre slashes open an enemy's face that tries to take advantage of Mayne's occupied state, and I run the last few steps, joining them in battle. "Safe. For now," Venom answers, as I flick my tail forward and land it square on the target before me. *Two lives.*

Steve grumbles low. "We should be protecting her, not this fucking dump." *I couldn't agree more.*

Ironside steps up to my side, with sick satisfaction on his leathery face and bloody fists raised in triumph to the sky. "Let them try to hurt her," he yells, victory already staining his baritone voice.

Sabre places his hand on Mayne's shoulder and says, "We should finish this lot and then defend Faun's position. There's no need for us to be separated."

With a nod of approval, Mayne plows into the last few males before us, ripping into them savagely. We move in to back him up quickly, attacking our foe swiftly, determined to get back to her as soon as we can.

I strike again. *Three.* And again. *Four.* In less than two minutes, the corridor is silent of all noise but our heavy breathing. My pack looks barely injured, minus a claw mark or two.

Venom turns back to where we came from and ushers us with his arm. "Hurry. I don't like that Faun and Tallon have been unguarded for so long."

As the close unit we are, we run together to find our woman and pack brother, our comradery stronger than ever.

Venom points to the storage door that contains them with a curse, because Sylva, Adda, and King are forcefully trying to push in the ajar entrance.

With an epic roar, Mayne succeeds in claiming their full attention, and they turn to face us with a mixture of fury and barely concealed fear. They may be tough, but they're nothing compared to the combined power of my brothers and me.

Venom and I slide our bodies in front of the door, positioning ourselves as their last defense, lest they manage to get through the huge beasts now pummeling their asses into the ground. Though, I highly doubt they'll be able to at this point.

Adda perishes first at the hands of Steve, who rips her head clean off before she even knows what hit her. Ironside takes out King, decimating him until he is nothing more than pieces of what used to be. That leaves Mayne and Sabre to battle Sylva together, our chosen leaders against theirs. Unfortunately for Sylva, it's clear that he's no match for combined agility and power, and his roars of pain echo through the halls before silence reigns once more. Watching the wet plonk of his fetid heart as it splats to the ground from Sabre's grip is the last moment we waste on their malicious lives. No more will they hurt our family, or anyone else's, for that matter.

It almost seems anticlimactic, after all the years of trouble they've given us and all the lives they've taken, but at the end of the day, they were just mortal people like us, their lives as fleeting as our own. The only difference is that their time is over now, and we remain.

Guns pop off around us and a bullet grazes along my arm, making me yelp in pain. The slicing burn has me saying between clenched teeth, as I hold my bleeding bicep, "We need to get out of here."

The door behind me suddenly opens, and Venom almost falls back as he was leaning on it. "Get your asses in here," Tallon cries, grabbing my good arm. "All of you. Quick."

We scurry inside, the room too small for comfort with such large bodies in its confine. Without a word, we surround Faun, placing her in the center of our bodies because protecting her is an unspoken necessity that drives us constantly.

Ironside moves some furniture in front of the door, blocking the exit from any unwanted intruder, and I breathe in slowly, not wanting to let the rapidly growing hot air make me feel as stifling as it clearly is.

FAUN

Why is this happening?

The scent of freshly spilled blood lingers in the air around me, and I try not to gag as anxiety fills my heart, wondering what horrors my males have been through already today.

It's been reasonably quiet outside, with the odd sound of fighting coming and going. Clearly, though, none of us have any desire to leave our cocoon of sanctuary any time soon.

We hunker quietly in the small room, every now and then a different one of them stroking my skin softly as if to make sure I'm still there and still alright. I understand the feeling because the fear mounting in me is escalating to an unfathomable height, as my heart pounds against my chest. It's not even me I'm scared for, it's them. I can't lose even one of them without my world splintering into a thousand pieces.

Alfa. My Broken wolf comes to mind, and the idea that I have no idea what's happening to him while all this is going on is freaking terrifying. What if someone attacked him in the medical bay? What if he needs me, and I'm sitting here in a closet hiding?

Tears prick my eyes, and I inhale slowly, focussing on staying calm. If I freak out now, things will only get worse. All I can do is keep my shit together and hope to God that we somehow make it out of this unscathed.

A heavy pounding beats against the closet door, making me jump. A small squeal pops right out of my mouth without permission, and I slam my hands over it to stop any more from escaping as the pounding continues.

I hear scraping as someone moves the furniture blocking the door, and the males between me and it maneuver me to be against the back wall, sheltering me from the incoming storm, whatever it may be.

Ironside rips open the door suddenly, and I squeeze my eyes closed and scream through my fingers, my mouth betraying me again.

I hear Mayne roar with fury, his body no doubt ready to pounce, but nothing happens, and I peel my frightened eyes open.

"Alfa?" Sabre's voice sounds both confused and hopeful.

I move back and forth, trying to see what's going on beyond the giant bodies obstructing my view, but with no use.

I hear Morigan say, "Hey fellas, how about we get out of here while the getting's good? Where's Faun?"

The males around me part and I squeeze through, finding Alfa in between both Dr. Adinases, his weight very much being held up by the two, but all I can focus on is his golden eyes locked on mine and a sob rips from my throat, relief flooding me.

It takes everything I have not to jump on him there and then, but he's clearly still weak and healing from Adda's attack on him.

Speaking of Adda, I look down at the bodies strewn across the floor outside our hidey-hole and see the gruesome remains of not just her, but Sylva and King, too. I flick my gaze away, not wanting to see it. They may have been my enemies in this life, but I would never revel in another person's demise—only sadness for their loss fills me now. Sadness for the only life they'll ever know.

"Hey, my love," Alfa greets me and I step forward, delicately kissing his furry cheek. "Did you miss me? Because I missed you like crazy."

A tear tracks down my face, and I smile through my wet vision. "So very much. Don't you ever scare me like that again."

"I hate to interrupt this lovely moment, but this guy is heavy as heck, and I'm not exactly young anymore. A little help," Dr. Foster Adina says with a strained voice, and I notice his puffed breaths and sweaty forehead for the first time. "Also, we've gotta get out of here. It's now or never because they've just given the formal go-ahead to terminate the program."

Ironside and Steve swing in and take Alfa off their hands, supporting him without any effort, telling him how happy they are that he's okay at the same time.

Nanuk grabs me and lifts me onto his back. "Hold on. I won't be happy unless I have you against me, pretty girl." I want to disagree because I'm technically faster than most of the people here, but I don't have the heart to say no to that because I feel it too, the need for touch and comfort.

I wrap my arms and legs around his large body and kiss his neck. "Let's go, baby."

We start to run as a group, the need for words absent because we know instinctively what we need to do. We've been together for so long that strategy is unnecessary. We know how to protect our own.

The males of my pack that aren't holding someone up surround us, with our leaders in the front with Dr. Foster Adina as he shows the way he wants us to go to escape this wretched place. Morigan stays with us in the center, her vulnerability obvious in what is now a land of unruly beasts.

The elder Dr. Adina opens doors with ease, using his fingerprint and scanning his eyes as we go, and before we know it, we're in hallways that we've never seen before, passing windows that look outside. The *actual* outside!

I try not to get too distracted by the rows and rows of trees and endless green grass, needing to pay attention to my closer surroundings because at any time a threat could appear, and we need to be ready.

Behind me, Alfa gasps, and I turn to see him being carried by his pack brothers and staring out beyond the windows. "It's beautiful."

I couldn't agree more. It is beautiful, and soon it will be ours, and we will be finally free.

CHAPTER 28
FAUN

Dr. Foster Adina opens a door on the left and ushers us inside, where we find a cement stairwell going down.

"Hurry," he insists as we pile in. "At the bottom, there's another door. When you open it, run like hell and don't stop or separate in case you get lost. The woods are just beyond, and I have secured a place that we can hide, but it's quite a far run, so I hope you ate your breakfast this morning because you're going to need the energy."

Just then, shouting and the pounding of steps start to get closer, and my ears twitch. "Run," I say, they're coming.

I slip down off Nanuk's back and grab Morigan's hand, and we start to sprint down the steps, her father close behind us and Nanuk now in the rear, keeping us safe. I'm not going as fast as I'd like because the humans are much slower than we are.

Sabre opens the bottom door and runs alongside his pack brothers as they heft Alfa into the woods beyond, disappearing into it as we emerge.

"We need to run faster," Nanuk grumbles.

I agree. "Take Morigan and run with Styng and Tallon. Mayne

and I will stay with Dr. Foster Adina and catch up. Go," I demand, pointing into the thicket of trees.

Nanuk sweeps her up without a warning, and they run off. I'm so glad that my pack trusts my instincts and isn't fighting me on what I'm saying.

I turn to tell Mayne to pick up the older doctor, but a spray of bullets rains down on us through the still open door as a couple of guards race down the stairwell to stop our escape.

We dive to the ground and I get a mouthful of dirt. *Fuck. That was close.* I think to myself as I scramble back to my knees. I turn to tell the other two to run, but my eyes widen as I take in the still and bloody form of Dr. Adina. His eyes are closed, but his chest is still rising.

Without pause, Mayne sweeps him up into his arms and takes off like the wildcat that he is, bounding beyond the treeline for safety with me hot on his heels, my eyelids burning from unshed tears, fearing for our savior's life.

I pass Mayne easily and catch up to the others. Morigan is pointing in the direction that we need to go as she piggybacks on Nanuk's back.

"We just have to keep following the compass in this direction, and we should come across a flashing red light because we've activated it. It'll be some time before we come across it, though," Morigan explains. "Do you need to put me down?" she asks Nanuk, concern lacing her voice.

He laughs and keeps running, focused on the destination. "Not at all. You're as light as a feather."

She scoffs. "That's the first time anyone's ever said that to me. I'm not exactly the smallest of women. Where's dad?" she asks me as I sprint beside them, not in the slightest bit tired from the effort.

Refusing to look up at her, I pick up my pace and call back. "Mayne has him. They're coming." There's no freaking way I'm worrying her before we can get to safety. Plus, how can I tell her that he's been shot? *I'm such a coward.*

Night starts to fall as we continue our run to the safe haven that awaits us. Steve, Ironside, Alfa, Venom, and Mayne stay behind us, losing their momentum, but Nanuk, Sabre, and I keep powering through in the front, knowing that the others can easily track our scent.

The darkness lingers on for what feels like forever, until I notice a small red light flashing in the distance, just like Morigan described earlier. I let the others know I see it, and Sabre says he'll wait here for the others and direct them where to go, and make sure they've all made it safely.

The pit of my stomach drops as I think of Morigan's father. *I hope he's okay.* As soon as we get inside, I'll tell her, so she's prepared for when they get here.

We approach the light, and Nanuk drops Morigan to the ground carefully before cracking his back and stretching.

She and I walk over to it, but I can clearly see that she is having trouble seeing in the dark as she carefully drops to her knees and waves her hands around like she's looking for something.

"What do you need?" I ask, wanting to help. "I can see pretty well at the moment."

Morigan sits back on her heels and smiles into the darkness. "There should be a lever hiding amongst the leaves near the light somewhere. It's made of wood and looks like a branch."

I look around and touch pieces of wood until I find what she's describing, and when I try to pull up the stick, it only moves slightly. A click sounds as a hatch just beyond it opens up, the top of it camouflaged with fallen leaves and dirt as though it's just a part of the ground. *Very impressive.*

A dull orange light comes from the hole and I look down to see a ladder that goes underground. Morigan leans in next to me before she speaks. "Well done. You won't be able to stay there long, just long enough for me and dad to return with the van, so we can ferry you all out of here without being seen."

She turns around and starts to lower herself down, and I nod for

Nanuk to follow after her. "I'll wait up here," I tell him, and he hesitates. "If I hear anything dodgy at all, I'll come in and close the door. I promise. I need to be here to meet the others."

Understanding shines in his eyes, knowing that I need to see for myself if the others are safe, and he lowers himself down the ladder with Morigan.

I look over to see Sabre watching me in the distance, his feline eyes shining in the darkness beyond. I'm not worried because I know I'm not alone out here. Sabre would never let anything happen to me.

Venom and Styng are the first to arrive. Styng's arm has now been wrapped up to stop the bleeding from the gunshot he got earlier. I kiss them both thoroughly, glad they got here safe, before watching them disappear below. Thankfully, Ironside, Alfa, and Steve aren't far behind them. Alfa looks a bit better than he did before, and it makes me smile.

"See, you were worried about nothing," Alfa tells me with a wink, as he lowers himself down the ladder. I make sure that Steve goes down before him in case he slips, but his descent is smooth, and I sigh in relief as Ironside wraps his arms around me.

He kisses me in between my antlers and says, "Everyone will be okay." I know he's trying to reassure me, but that's because he didn't see what I did.

"Where's Tallon?" I ask, knowing he was with them the last time I saw him.

Ironside looks back into the darkness that he came from with a frown. "Mayne and Dr. Adina were taking a long time to catch up to us, so he decided to wait and see if they needed extra help in the dark. It seems odd that it was taking them so long, considering how slow *we* were going." I shake my head and look down, my gut-wrenching. "What's wrong?" he asks me worriedly.

"It's the doctor," I whisper quietly. "He was shot as we were escaping. I haven't had the heart to tell Morigan. He was alive the last time I saw him, but... It looked bad. There was a lot of blood."

Sabre approaches us, hearing what I told Ironside. "It's only right to warn her, Faun."

"I know."

"I'll take care of it for you, sweetheart. I don't want you to have to do that," Sabre says, taking my face in his hands and kissing me softly. "You stay up here with Ironside and holler if you need help with him when they get here."

With one last lingering look into the woods, Sabre sighs with sadness and goes to do what I was too chickenshit to do. I'm so grateful for his strength right now because I feel like I'm barely holding on.

Another half an hour passes as Ironside and I sit beside the hatch, listening to Morigan's sobs from below. *Please hurry, Mayne.*

As if my plea conjures him from the depths of the night, Tallon and Mayne carrying Dr Adina stroll through the trees, the thick scent of fresh blood tingeing the air and making me sick all over again.

"Is he?" I can't finish my question as I stand, scared of what I'm going to be told, but Mayne smiles weakly at me to reassure me, knowing what I mean.

A croaked voice comes from his back. "I'm still alive."

I suck in a breath at the pained voice, and Ironside plucks him carefully off Mayne's back. "Let's get you downstairs, sir."

With careful movements, he holds the doctor close to his chest with one arm and uses the other to make his way down the ladder, and I slump in Tallon's hold as he wraps his arms around me.

"He doesn't have long," Tallon whispers in my ear, and my heart plummets. "We got him here as fast as we could, but there were a few scares along the way. I'm sorry."

Mayne wraps an arm around the both of us, and we just stand there in each other's embrace as a cry of pain slips from Morigan's lips and I wince, letting my own tears flow unchecked. This man has risked everything for us, and now it seems he'll die for us too. My heart breaks, guilt and grief choking me.

I break away from the hug and know it's time to face the music whether I want to or not, because no one can ever be truly ready for something like this. It's an unavoidable part of life that makes your own wants and needs no longer seem important when faced with the death of someone you love or care about. Saying goodbye has never felt more painful, and knowing there's nothing I can do about it, even more so.

Each step down strangles me further, and when I reach the platform, I turn to face all my other males sitting quietly at the other end of the room in respect as Morigan cradles her father's head in her lap, rocking back and forth, sobbing as he weakly hugs her and whispers words of love.

Mayne and Tallon come up beside me, kissing my cheek on each side before silently and respectfully joining their pack brothers.

I step forward and kneel beside Morigan's trembling body and look down at her honorable father. "Thank you," I tell him, needing him to know that his sacrifice is both appreciated and won't be taken for granted. "You have given us life and freedom. I'm so sorry this has happened to you." My voice breaks at the end, and I wipe away a cascade of tears that I can't seem to be able to wrangle. "Without you, we would be dead, or worse. You're the closest thing to a father that we'll ever have. I wish we had more time."

Morigan puts her arm around me and pulls me in closer as Foster says weakly, "I remember holding your little hand when you were born and swearing to protect you. You felt like another daughter, and it's because of you that I saw the truth," he splutters and coughs up some blood, wheezing deeply. "Keep each other safe and live well. You know what you need to do, my darling girl," he says to Morigan before closing his eyes, his breath becoming more ragged and uneven. "I'm so proud of you."

Dr. Foster Adina, my ultimate protector, takes his last pained breath and his friendly face goes lax. Morigan rips out a scream of protest, and I wrap my arms around her as we sob together over his body. My heart splinters for my friend.

Time passes as we mourn together, tears shed from every one of us in our underground safe house. Probably too much time, but none of us really care because his life is worth so much more than just merely moving on with our day.

Styng finds us some water bottles and snacks, insisting that we consume them to keep up our energy. We nap, we drink, and we cry more before Morigan stands up, wiping her saturated face with the sleeve of her work shirt.

"We can't stay down here." Her voice is hollow, but her eyes harden with determination. "Dad wouldn't want us to stop now, not after we've come so far."

This woman impresses me more every minute. The pain and anguish she's feeling aren't even enough to slow down her selfless heart.

"What do you need us to do?" Steve asks with his head high, ready to be called into action.

Morigan looks him up and down before eyeing up the rest of us and landing on Nanuk. "You are with me, big fella. With a pair of glasses and your hands in your pocket, you could probably pass for human if you stay far enough away from them. I need to go and pick up our vehicle and bring it back here." She turns back to me. "Stay inside until we get back. You need to remain quiet as well, just in case they manage to bring a search party this far out."

I nod in understanding and practically jump in Nanuk's arms. "Keep safe and take care of Morigan," I tell him before smothering his face in kisses.

Before long, the hatch closes behind them, and I get a sinking feeling in my stomach. *Please come back to me.*

Styng calls me over to his little makeshift bed and I join him, turning my back toward him and wiggling back into his warm embrace so that he's my big spoon, and I let my tears fall again.

In the last few days, I've cried more than I have in years. The only saving grace from all this shit is the men that surround me, loving me endlessly and filling me with hope for a happy future.

I fall asleep in Styng's arms, with my mind on tomorrow and the longing for happiness to come.

CHAPTER 29
IRONSIDE

I SIT IN QUIET REFLECTION AT THE BOTTOM OF THE LADDER, next to the late Dr. Adina, and look over at my sleeping pack. The conflicting emotions inside me rail against my mind.

As happy as I am that we're free and outside, it feels wrong now because of the sacrifice made for that very freedom. Is it worth the world losing such a great, noble man? Morigan losing her father? From this moment on, I'll make it worth it. I will live every day to its potential and appreciate every breath of fresh air.

Sighing, I look down at the good doctor. "We will give you a proper burial, my friend." I keep my voice low, not wanting to wake the others. It's been a long couple of days, and they need their rest.

A tapping from the hatch above garners my immediate attention, and my whole body tenses as I turn and get into a crouched position, poised to attack any unwanted visitors that may have found us.

Sunshine beams down as the hatch opens, and I have to shield my eyes from the sudden blinding light. Before I get a chance to go on the offensive, Nanuk's scent floats down as he says, "It's just us."

I relax my body and start the climb up to them. Pulling myself easily over the edge, I take in the haggard, tired appearance of Morigan, and sadness on her behalf envelops me.

Without a word, I step past Nanuk and open my arms for her. Morigan steps into my embrace with a sob and buries her face in my chest, letting out all of her grief and loss. Nanuk joins the others downstairs as I comfort Morigan, giving her all the time she needs.

My heart aches for her and for the fact that if it wasn't for us, he would still be here. The guilt of her dad's death will carry with me forever. We might not have been directly responsible, but that doesn't make me feel any better.

The rest of my pack remains below, not making a sound, undoubtedly hearing the wrenching sobs ripped from Morigan. When she calms herself back down and all that's left is trembling inhales, Faun pops her head up with a sad smile.

"Can I get you anything?" she asks with concern, her own eyes wet with silent tears as she looks at Morigan.

"No. Well... yes, actually," she replies to Faun. "I can't leave my father like that. Can you ask your pack if they'll help to put him to rest? It's what he'll want, and we can't stay here any longer. It's not safe."

The strength of this human is astounding. Regardless of her understandable grief, she still wants to press forward and save us all. My respect for Morigan grows even more, and I vow to always be there for her whenever she needs us.

"Why are you doing all of this for us?" I ask, unable to tamper my curiosity.

Morigan straightens her crumpled work outfit and wipes her tears away as resolve joins with the hurt in her eyes. "My father felt extraordinarily responsible for not only your unfavorable living conditions but also for your very existence; and he looked upon you all, most especially your pack, as his extended children," she starts to explain as Faun wraps an arm around her shoulder. "From as young as I can remember, he would tell me fairy stories of a little faun princess trapped in a mighty dungeon with all of her special friends;

and that one day a healer would come along and set them all free, so they could live happily ever after. It wasn't until I was much older that I realized the truth, and he sat down and explained it to me and told me of his guilt and the importance of him doing the right thing. Straight away, I knew what I had to do, and I had no doubt that I wanted to help him fulfill his dreams."

"I started to angle my studies to follow in his footsteps, and before long I was at the Ark. I had mixed feelings when I started to mingle with the Broken inside; on one hand I was nervous about letting loose such a vicious set of people, who seemed to relish in the pain and misery of others, but on the other hand, I met your pack, and I knew it wasn't right." Morigan looks hard at Faun, and I know our beautiful female won her over in the end.

"Aren't you wishing that you didn't help us now? After what happened with your dad?" Faun asks, shifting her feet nervously.

Morigan's gaze drifts away slightly, and fresh tears silently spill down her cheeks. "No, because I know that wherever he is, my dad is at peace knowing that you got out of there and that it was all worth it. As much as I'd like to be selfish and wish it was all different, I would never take away his honor like that. It meant so much to him and I will see his dreams through to the end, no matter what it takes. I will get you to your new home safely."

I've never thought very highly of humans because of how they've treated us over the years, but Morigan and Foster give me hope that this world has tremendous good in it. "Thank you," I tell her simply, because there is nothing more I can say that would ever express what her sacrifice means to me, to *us*.

Faun and Morigan take a slow stroll through the woods with me trailing a respectful distance behind them, as the rest of our pack puts Dr. Foster Adina to rest, not far from the hatch. Morigan said she couldn't be a part of it because it hurt too much, and that she would say goodbye to him once they were done. The agony she must be feeling has us all somber, and the mood around us all is heavy and quiet, out of respect for them both.

When the time comes for Morigan to say her final goodbye, we all gather downstairs to give her some privacy, with Mayne on the ladder listening out for any potential threats, and I wrap Faun up in my arms as I pull her into my lap.

"You may be big and scary, Ironside, but you're also one of the kindest males I've ever known. I'm so proud to call you mine." Her soft, sad eyes look up at me, and I'm once again blown away by how much love I feel for this female. I would do absolutely anything just to make her smile. She is my whole life, and it brings me joy knowing that I'm not the only one that feels that way.

CHAPTER 30
FAUN

WE PILE INTO A PLAIN, UNMARKED WHITE VAN WITH HEAVILY tinted windows awaiting us in the secluded parking lot, next to a walking trail leading back into the woods we just appeared from, and I look back into the trees with a sad sort of feeling.

While I'm looking forward to seeing what is in store for my future, the Ark is all I've ever known, and the home that made me who I am today. I say goodbye to my past and the closest man that I'll ever have to a father and squeeze into the van, sitting between Venom and Alfa, who is a million times better than he was yesterday. His sweet smile always shines brightly for me.

The drive Morigan takes us on carries on for the whole day, with us only stopping for the occasional toilet breaks in the most desolate stops she can find. I thought that being in a car for the first time would be fun, but honestly, I just feel really sick and spend most of the journey trying not to throw up.

I don't know why humans love these contraptions so much.

Eventually, we stop at a small dingy hotel in some out-of-the-way country town, and Morigan gets out to rent us some rooms to stay in for the night. There's no way we can all sleep in this van; it's squished enough as it is without us trying to lie down in it.

When she returns, she tells us that she only got two rooms, not wanting to pull any suspicion or attention our way. Which is frankly fine with me because I wasn't going to let any of my males out of my sight, anyway.

After backing the car as close to the hotel door as possible, she opens it, and then the van door, quickly ushering us from one to the other as she looks around nervously, hoping that there's no one around to see us because there's no doubt we'd stand out with our animal-like features.

Keeping the light off, we bundle in together. Morigan puts her head in the door. "Will you guys be alright in here?" she asks, and we agree quickly. "Good. Then I'll be just next door if you need me. We shouldn't have any issues. These rooms are so far away from the road and any other areas of interest, and it's not exactly a tourist spot by the looks of it; but just to be safe, stay inside and set the alarm for four am. I want to get out of here before anyone else wakes up."

I listen carefully after she closes our door to her, locking the van and entering her own room, and I don't relax until I hear her shower start up.

Letting out a big breath, I flop back onto the bed and close my eyes, thinking of how lucky we are to have made it this far.

Sabre's scent envelops me as he lies beside me on the bed, moving my hair off my cheek before kissing my neck softly. "We're so close. Can you feel it?"

I smile as heat rises within me and a sudden need that I wasn't prepared for; the accumulation of his soft touch and the last few crazy days overwhelms me. All I can think of is how lucky I am and how much I must have them all close to me.

Opening my eyes, I look up at Sabre's strong angular face, golden eyes, and elongated teeth, and know what I need.

I stand up and pull off my clothes in record time, while the males around me freeze, drinking in my every movement with a hunger I can feel to my core—my *throbbing* core.

Without an ounce of regret or nervousness, I lay on my back and spread my thighs wide, delighting in the sound of their breaths sucking in at my exposed body. I love how responsive they are to me now that they're no longer holding back their feelings or desires for me.

"I want you," I announce, looking between them. "All of you. I need to feel you all filling me, comforting me, loving me."

Steve growls low and practically rips his pants off before pouncing on me, his mouth between my thighs before anyone else even gets a chance to move.

"Fuck yes," he growls, then takes my clit into his mouth, sucking it down and licking my center like it's made from his favorite candy.

I cry out with my head flinging back, curses already on my lips before Styng covers my mouth with his, kissing me so thoroughly that I see stars, while a myriad of hands touch and stroke me, plucking at my sensitive nipples, not a hesitation to be heard.

Steve brings me to climax, quicker than I thought was possible, and almost immediately my hips are lifted high as he spears me hard and deep with his long girth.

"Oh, God, yes," I moan as Styng moves away from my mouth, only for more devouring kisses to come from Ironside.

Steve pounds into me with hard, unrelenting thrusts until I feel his body harden and tremble above me. As soon as he steps back, Sabre lies beside me rolling me on top of him until my back is on his front and Styng grabs my knees, spreading me wide and lifting them until Sabre places his hands under them, pulling higher until my pussy is open and utterly exposed.

"Stretch her," Sabre growls from underneath me. "Make her ready for me."

Without any hesitation, Styng kneels between my legs and places a finger inside me, pumping in and out, while Mayne uses a hand to circle my clit the way he knows I like. The wet sound from Steve's cum and my own juices fill the room as they work me over, but just before I climax, Styng removes his finger and rims my asshole with it, saturating me there too.

Mayne keeps rubbing my clit as Styng starts to work my ass over, inserting one and then two fingers inside, and it feels so fucking good that I beg for more, needing to detonate.

Sabre lets go of one of my legs and nudges my back package with his throbbing cock after Styng removes his fingers. "Yes," I plead, rolling my hips back to help him enter me.

With slow, careful movements, Sabre's cock slides into my ass and the fullness mixed with Mayne's ministrations has me screaming out and clenching around him.

"Fuuuck," Sabre moans in my ear, pushing deep inside me. "Your ass is so tight, baby."

Mayne moves back and Styng moves over me, lining his cock up with my pussy, and pushes into the wet mess with ease. Grunting in pleasure, he starts to move in and out of me, but when Sabre joins in with a matching rhythm, my eyes roll back in my head at how good it feels.

Someone grabs my antlers and moves my head to the side, away from Sabre, and I look up to see a naked and glorious Alfa above me. He tilts my head back and moves his hips forward, nudging my mouth with his cock, a bead of pre-cum already at the tip.

I lick it off, and he growls low. "Open your mouth and show me how much you missed me," he demands, his eyes dark with lust. I think I like this dominating side of him.

Happily complying, I tilt back further, loving his control on me, and suck his cock down all the way to the back of my throat as my other two males plow into me hard, pushing the head of his dick even further down until I gag on it.

"This is so fucking hot," Nanuk growls from somewhere beside us, but I focus on my body and all the sensations flowing over me.

Their rhythm starts to increase and become more frantic and Sabre suddenly digs his nails in as Styng curses loudly, the two of them spurting deep inside me at the same time as my pussy clenches with another mind-blowing orgasm.

Maybe I can't handle this. I think to myself, as my body trembles violently between them.

Styng and Sabre quietly move away as Tallon slides between my legs, taking my face in his hands. "Love you, precious," he says sweetly into my neck before thrusting his cock inside me, making me moan.

With deep slow strokes, his hips drive me into the mattress and the steady, maddening motion has me coming apart in minutes, clenching around him and bringing on his own release.

Alfa pulls his cock out of my mouth and lays back on the bed beside me. "My turn, but I've got to warn you, my love, I won't last long," he tells me, locking his gaze with mine.

Tallon kisses me softly, uncaring that I just had Alfa in my mouth before moving away. I shakily climb on top of Alfa, knowing he's probably too weak to be on top still.

I slide myself down on top of his cock and groan. I'm so fucking tender, but it feels too damn good to stop. I'm determined to have every one of my males empty inside me tonight. I *need* it.

Alfa grabs my hips as I slowly ride him, my legs struggling because they feel like jelly, but Ironside sits behind me, grasping my ass hard and bouncing me on top of Alfa, taking away the strain from my legs.

True to his word, Alfa roars soon after, emptying himself deep inside me, groaning and pinning me to him as his cock knots inside me. I stay seated for what feels like ages, but I happily kiss him softly, glad to have him safe and with me.

Alfa softens inside me at last, but before I can move, Ironside lifts me up off him and places me on my hands and knees facing the other direction, with Maynes awaiting cock near my mouth. Apparently, the wait was too long for some.

I eagerly open my lips and take him in, his salty taste as delicious as ever. I never knew I would love this so much, but I've found a deep satisfaction with having my strong males at my mercy while I devour them.

A dick pushes inside me from behind, and I pop Mayne out of my mouth briefly to look back into Venom's hooded eyes as his hips slowly roll in and out of me. My pussy's now a swollen, soaking wet mess, and I fucking love it!

Sucking Mayne back in, I groan deeply as he hits my throat at the same time that Venom pushes inside me with ferocity. They both swear at how good it feels to fill me, and they both start thrusting harder and deeper until I'm both gagging and moaning for more.

Mayne groans, gripping my antlers hard, "Hurry Venom, I'm gonna cum, and I want to do it in her tight cunt."

Instead of his vulnerable words shocking me, it just turns me on more as I roll my hips back with more force, wanting them both to lose themselves deep within me.

On cue, Venom grabs my hips harder and cries out, faltering his movements and just holding me hard against his own hips.

Mayne pulls out of my mouth and grabs his cock tightly as if he's in pain, pulling me away from Venom and dropping me into his lap, slipping inside me with a quick movement and cumming almost instantly with a guttural yell.

Nanuk sits next to him, patting his lap with a big grin. "Come, give me some of that sugar," he says with a cheeky grin, clearly excited to be inside me again.

I move onto his lap, and he pulls me in tight, using his big hands to grind me onto him over and over again. It feels like just the two of us as we kiss each other deeply, making love instead of fucking. It's intimate and beautiful, and when we orgasm together, it takes my breath away.

A deep, low chuckle reaches me, giving me goosebumps down my back as Ironside rumbles, "My turn."

Holy shit. Time for the big guns.

I slide off Nanuk carefully and turn to find Ironside stalking toward me with a predatory glint in his eyes. "If I'm ever gonna fit, it's gonna be now," he growls low, grabbing my feet suddenly and sliding me down the bed towards him, his gargantuan cock throbbing between his legs and pointing straight at its final destination.

I open my thighs wide and lean forward, grabbing him tightly, my fingers not meeting around him, and he moans. "Keep looking at me like that, and I'm gonna cum all over your hands."

I'm feeling bold as I pull him forward by it, and he lets me guide him down to my core. "Be gentle, big guy. I'd hate for you to break it."

"You know you can take me," Ironside replies slowly, rolling his hips as I guide him past my lips, his size already noticeable, but not in an altogether bad way. The pain and pleasure mix feels exquisite, and I push my pelvis higher, spearing him into me quicker than he was going for.

"Fuck," he swears, looking down at me with a tinge of worry, but I just do it again and again until Ironside takes back control, driving himself down to the hilt, and it's my turn to swear.

I pant slowly, and Ironside stays super still inside me, giving me time to get accommodated with his size. He brings his fingers between us and starts to strum my clit to the tune of pleasure, and all of a sudden I need more, rolling my hips in invitation.

Without a second to spare, Ironside slowly grinds in and out of me, while still bringing me closer to my happy ending with his talented digits. My arms pull him down close to me, and I kiss his wide chest, panting and groaning along with him.

The build-up becomes too much, and I let go, the whole world disappearing around me as I spasm all over, my pussy milking his dick of every drop as he gives himself to me completely with cried words of love.

My big male, always a sweetheart, even now.

Not wanting to squish me, Ironside slowly pulls himself out of me, rolling over, and I wince at the sting. My poor core is sorer than it's ever been, but also never more satisfied.

I close my eyes and smile, utter exhaustion immediately taking over. "I love you all, so much," I mumble with my eyes still closed, a yawn taking over at the end.

Someone lifts me up and rearranges me, laying my head on the pillows as one of my other males parts my legs, tenderly cleaning me with a warm damp towel. I cringe slightly but relax into it as it calms the ache.

I snuggle sideways when they're done and briefly recognize that I'm swaddled into a big chest as I let sleep take over. My heart is full and my hope for the future is guiding my dreams.

CHAPTER 31
FAUN

GETTING INTO THE VAN THE NEXT MORNING IS AN EXPERIENCE. Between my cowboy walk from the ache between my thighs, and the knowing glance that Morigan gives me as soon as I see her, I feel like disappearing into the ground. I'm so mortified and can't believe that I didn't even think about the fact that Morigan was just in the next room as I screamed for more cock. I can tell by Styng's chuckles as he watches me walk that he thinks it's bloody hilarious.

Morigan chuckles at my red cheeks and congratulates me for scoring such a *devoted* harem. *Kill me now.*

At least Morigan has a smile on her face this morning. If my utter embarrassment is all it takes, then I'm happy to take one—or nine—for the team.

My pack spends the day grinning from ear to ear while giving me hot glances, and I have a distinct feeling that it won't be the last time they ride the Faun choo-choo train. But it won't be for a while, because this girl needs a hot bath and a serious break to heal.

The car ride isn't anywhere near as long as yesterday, and before we know it, we're all quickly boarding onto a boat, sitting at a somewhat abandoned jetty after a long walk through a twisted overgrown path.

I was so terrified of being spotted by a human because there's no way in hell I can hide my two large antlers from anyone in the midday sun. Luckily, there was no one to be seen, and we ride out into the open sea, the wind rustling my hair messily around my head and tangling onto my antlers.

"This is incredible!" Steve yells out with his body half off the end of the boat, his hands skimming through the ocean waves that the boat makes as we speed along.

Mayne pulls him back up into the seat, growling. "Don't even think about jumping in there, Steve. The last thing we need is to be slowed down by you taking a dip. We'll be on an island, surrounded by water, just be fucking patient."

Steve grumbles incoherently, throwing out words like "It's Crush" and "I was only gonna be a minute."

I can't help the giggle that escapes me at his ridiculous notion of changing his name and how none of us will let him because, frankly, it's just too funny.

A dark shape rises up on the horizon, and Morigan points to it. "There she is, Freedom Island." I look over at her with a wide smile. "Dad thought you'd like that name," she adds on, her eyes taking on a sad shadow.

Standing up, I join her and put an arm around her shoulder as the boat bounces along. "Will you stay with us?" I ask, hoping that she'll say yes, but knowing she probably won't.

Not surprisingly, Morigan shakes her head. "I have a job lined up under my fake ID on the mainland, not far from the jetty, so that I can keep an eye out from there and make sure that your island stays safe and left alone. Plus, I think it's time you all embraced a life without the prying eyes of humans. Enjoy yourselves and let loose. I won't be far, and I'll visit so often that you'll probably get sick of me."

"You'd better." I fake scowl at her. "You're the only sister I have, after all." My words have her smiling again, and we look off towards the incoming island, and the beauty of it astounds me. "I can't believe this is our new home."

I turn to see my whole pack with eyes riveted on Freedom Island and I know our life will never be the same again, but for the first time in a long time, I feel truly safe. Ironside notices me watching them and blows me a quick kiss; it still surprises me that there's so much gooey inside all that gruff.

When the boat stops at a makeshift jetty that they must have put together for this very purpose, Steve and Nanuk dive straight into the water while the rest of us carefully disembark, moving to the more stable rocky shoreline.

The hot sun kisses my cheeks as I close my eyes and lean my head back, feeling the soft salty breeze caressing me lovingly. It feels like the island is whispering "Welcome home", and my heart stutters in my chest as hot tears burn under my lids.

"Come on, I'll show you the base camp that we've managed to put together for you," Morigan tells us, loud enough to catch Steve and Nanuk's attention as well.

We follow her down a small path between some trees for a minute or so until we come to a clearing. It seems to have the basic necessities, from a fire pit in the center, jugs, and baskets with cooking and eating supplies, everything we'd need for fishing and hunting, a large cubby house filled with pillows, blankets, and some clothes, and other bits and pieces here and there. Sabre excitedly goes through everything.

"I know it's nothing flashy, but it was all we could do on such short notice without drawing attention to ourselves, but anything you need that you don't have, I can easily bring over from the mainland in my monthly visits. Just give me a list, and I'll do what I can. My dad had a very good nest egg put aside and now that he's..." Morigan chokes on her words for a minute before continuing, "not here anymore, it'll all be coming to me. Money won't be an issue, thankfully."

Her somber features pull at my heartstrings and I ask, "Do you want to camp with us tonight?"

Morigan politely declines, telling us that she has people to meet and needs to organize her own place and meet her new bosses first thing in the morning. She reminds us to stay inside the tree line if any boats come by, but that we should be okay because it's very well known that the island is covered with endangered venomous snakes and spiders. She winks at Venom and he grins in response.

"I'll make sure to bring my medical kit with me each time I come over here. I did leave a mini one in your cubby though, in case of injury, and there's a satellite phone as well with my number beside it. Only use it for emergencies," Morigan tells us with a serious face. "I'll redo your birth control shot every quarter, as usual, so you won't have to worry about any surprises."

Steve snorts a laugh. "Can you imagine a half crocodile and half deer kid?" He laughs even harder, bending at the waist. "No, thank you. We have enough problems as it is."

We join in, laughing along at the idea because even though I'm sure kids are great, they're not something that's on any of our minds. It would be selfish for me to bring a child into the world without genes. Who knows what damage that could do? If we can even procreate, anyway.

"What do you think happened with the Broken we left behind?" I ask her, even though I'm afraid of the answer.

With a sigh, Morigan says, "I have no idea, but considering I know that Dr. Micheals wasn't at work when the riots happened, I have no doubt he'll be working on phase two."

We sit and contemplate that for a while in silence, but at the end of the day, there's nothing we can do now, except hope that he gets shut down before it's too late.

Walking Morigan back to her boat, we joke and laugh about all of our possibilities, but as we reach the shore, Morigan and I stop and look out at the horizon as the guys goof around on the sand, diving in and out of the water like giant children. All except for Alfa, who lies back on the sand with a smile. No doubt he's still recovering from his near-death experience.

"There will never be enough words to tell you how thankful I am that you saved us, or how sorry I am that it cost you your dad," I tell Morigan as we lean into each other, nudging our shoulders together.

She turns and smiles at me. "I have no doubt in my mind that he's watching over us with tears in his eyes, never regretting his choice for even a second." Morigan breathes out a heavy sigh and looks toward the boat. "It's time for me to go and you to live. All I ask is that you find happiness every day and that you all love each other fully. That's how I want you to show me how thankful you are. Be free, my friend. Be free."

With that, she walks away and climbs into her boat, taking off into the sunset with a small wave as leaves.

I look back at my nine devoted, loving, strong males and smile so wide that it hurts my cheeks. Tallon waves wildly at me with a smile as wide as my own, his scars on full display without a care in the world, and I know everything is going to be alright from now on.

Thank you, Foster. For everything.

ACKNOWLEDGMENTS

Grandma, because of you my world is filled with unending imagination, stories that flow like a river, and the courage to know that I count for something in this world. Without your love and guidance I wouldn't be who I am today and there are no words to tell you how much you mean to me for that. I can't imagine my world without you in it but I endeavour to always be the best version of myself that I can be because of you.

Grandad, you are the greatest man I have ever had the privilege of knowing. You are the strongest, kindest, most intelligent man who has never let me down, and you've shown me what a real man is meant to be. You have been a role model my whole life and I aspire to be even half the person you are. The absolute unyielding love you have shown Grandma every single day is awe worthy. You are a truly great man with a truly great heart. Even though you don't approve of my choice of profession, I know that you will always be proud of me regardless.

A big thank you to my hubby, wife, and spawn of my loins. Your love means more to me than anything else in the world. There are no words that will ever be good enough to express my love for you.

Thank you to my family and friends for always having my back and supporting me in all of my endeavours. It's very much appreciated.

A shout out especially to Tash, Jade, Sandy, Claire, and any one else who helped me get through my recent tough times while writing this book. For a bit there, it seemed like I was never going to get it out with my life fighting me all the way but having support made all the difference.

To Charlotte, thank you for all of the time and energy you put into helping me to better understand the crazy Indie world.

Branka, Lola, and Bobbi; I miss you guys every day.

Ashleigh, Rebecca and Jen, we are in dire need for a catch up. You ladies always give me the feeling of home.

My alpha/beta readers, thank you for being the first people to tell me where I've fucked up. You ladies keep me from embarrassing myself. Thank you.

Hmm... I think I forgot someone...

Psych! Amanda, love ya bitch! You are the absolute shit and stuck with me forever. I am so grateful for every single motha fuckin thing you do. You help me get through all the shit, even when both Brian's have pissed off at the pub. You kept me sane through this whole stage of my life and I would be legit screwed without you. BTW, there are sooo many drinks in our future.

ABOUT THE AUTHOR

Hi, I'm Alexandra, an Aussie/Kiwi mother of three, married to the best husband around.

My life is surrounded by lots of animals because I just can't say no to all their cuteness. I have a rare chronic illness that keeps me grateful for the beauty that life brings, and my pen name is in honour of my amazing Grandparents who are everything to me.

My soul lives off coffee, family, reading, storms, good scotch and great wine, mountains, and is a real knowledge whore.

I'm a firm believer in being kind to others because it *does* matter, and it *does* make a difference. If I can make just one person happy with my stories, or even give them a reprieve they may desperately need to escape their harder reality, then I've done my job right.

My imagination is a constantly growing paradise for me and I feel blessed that I get to share a little of it with you.

Thank you for coming on my journey with me; You *are* appreciated.

If you have enjoyed my story, please take the time to leave me a review on amazon. Reviews are the bread and butter of indy authors and every one counts.

Here are some links to my social media accounts:

Facebook Group:
https://www.facebook.com/groups/alexandrasguardians

Facebook Page:

https://www.facebook.com/Alexandra.K.Martin.Books

Amazon:

https://www.amazon.com/Alexandra-K-Martin/e/B08NHK4JC4/

Instagram:

https://instagram.com/alexandra.k.martin.books?igshid=1m508hfimy8zz

Goodreads:

https://www.goodreads.com/author/show/20962962.Alexandra_K_Martin

Newsletter

https://mailchi.mp/27cd881447ed/alexandrakm-nl

Tiktok:

https://vm.tiktok.com/ZSeM3U4HQ/

Website:

https://intriguingauthorpa.com/authors/alexandra.html

OTHER BOOKS BY ALEXANDRA K. MARTIN

Series

Rathe Chronicles (Epic Fantasy Romance)

-Summer's Confine, Book One (RH)

-Janice's Entanglement, Book Two (Menage)

-Havana's Hell, Book Three (MF)

-Alice's Coalition, Book Four (RH/Coming soon)

Depths of Mitchelton High Trilogy (Contemporary Dark Bully Academy RH)

-Payne (Coming soon)

Standalones/ Collaborative Standalones

-Lust: A Golden Bird Retelling. Sinners Fairytales Collaboration, Book Six (Dark Contemporary RH)

-Broken Faun (Sci-Fi RH)

Anthologies

-Hidden Fate (menage), featured in 'Rebirth of the Dark Hunter' (Urban Fantasy)

-Dom X (MF), featured in 'My Perfect Pleasure' (Erotic/ Coming May 2022) CO-WRITE as SOUL SISTERS

-Releasing the Beast, featured in 'Voices of the night' (Horror/ Coming July 2022) CO-WRITE as SOUL SISTERS

CHECK OUT SOUL SISTERS

Coming May 2022. Dom X, in My Perfect Pleasure (Soul Sisters)

Pre-order link: https://tinyurl.com/MyPerfectPleasure

CHECK OUT JAY LEIGH BROWN

Looking for new books to read? Try Ruined by Rubies from Jay Leigh Brown

CHECK OUT JAY LEIGH BROWN

http://bit.ly/RuinedByRubiesJLB

www.ingramcontent.com/pod-product-compliance
Lightning Source LLC
Chambersburg PA
CBHW020516120726
47904CB00003B/854